Dear Rea...

I'm plea... THE DEVERAUX
LEGACY... ton, South
Carolina, the books follow the fortunes of the Deveraux
family.

Grace and Tom Deveraux divorced years ago—for reasons
known only to them. Both have regrets, as well as a deep
and abiding love for each other, and they worry their own
foolhardy actions have permanently affected their children.
More than anything, Grace and Tom want their children to
avoid their mistakes and have the kind of enduring, happy
marriages of which dreams—and families—are made. Both
are equally skeptical it will ever happen, however, since...

Chase, the oldest son and magazine publisher spends his
time advising his male readers how to be happy—with or
without a wife. Mitch, an innovative businessman and the
second-born son, who will one day take his father's place at
the helm of the Deveraux Shipping Company, has already
weathered a divorce of his own and is now willing to consider
marriage as a business deal. Third-born Gabe, a doctor and
the Good Samaritan of the family, is contemplating siring a
baby as a favor for one of his lady friends! Only Amy, the
baby of the family and owner of her own interior design
business, wants it all—love, romance and children—the
old-fashioned, time-honored way.

Eventually, of course, all the Deveraux siblings will find
happiness, and the love, passion and romance they have been
waiting for. And perhaps a little of life's wisdom along the
way...

Best wishes,

Cathy Gillen Thacker

Dear Reader,

Welcome to Harlequin American Romance, where you're guaranteed heartwarming, emotional and deeply romantic stories set in the backyards, big cities and wide-open spaces of America. Kick starting the month is Cathy Gillen Thacker's *Her Bachelor Challenge*, which launches her brand-new family-connected miniseries THE DEVERAUX LEGACY. In this wonderful story, a night of passion between old acquaintances has a sought-after playboy businessman questioning his bachelor status.

Next, Mollie Molay premieres her new GROOMS IN UNIFORM miniseries. In *The Duchess & Her Bodyguard*, protecting a royal beauty was easy for a by-the-book bodyguard, but falling in love wasn't part of the plan! Don't miss *Husbands, Husbands…Everywhere!* by Sharon Swan, in which a lovely B & B owner's ex-husband shows up on her doorstep with amnesia, giving her the chance to rediscover the man he'd once been. This poignant reunion romance story is the latest installment in the WELCOME TO HARMONY miniseries. Laura Marie Altom makes her Harlequin American Romance debut with *Blind Luck Bride*, which pairs a jilted groom with a pregnant heroine in a marriage meant to satisfy the terms of a bet.

This month, and every month, come home to Harlequin American Romance—and enjoy!

Best,

Melissa Jeglinski
Associate Senior Editor
Harlequin American Romance

Cathy Gillen Thacker

HER BACHELOR CHALLENGE

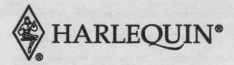

HARLEQUIN®

TORONTO • NEW YORK • LONDON
AMSTERDAM • PARIS • SYDNEY • HAMBURG
STOCKHOLM • ATHENS • TOKYO • MILAN • MADRID
PRAGUE • WARSAW • BUDAPEST • AUCKLAND

This book is dedicated to David and Meredith Thacker,
who have found in each other everything they have always
wanted. I couldn't be happier about your marriage.
I wish you much love and joy in your new life together.

ISBN 0-373-16937-X

HER BACHELOR CHALLENGE

Copyright © 2002 by Cathy Gillen Thacker.

Visit us at www.eHarlequin.com

Printed in U.S.A.

ABOUT THE AUTHOR

Cathy Gillen Thacker married her high school sweetheart and hasn't had a dull moment since. Why, you ask? Well, there were three kids, various pets, any number of automobiles, several moves across the country, his and her careers, and sundry other experiences. But mostly, there was love and friendship and laughter, and lots of experiences she wouldn't trade for the world.

You can find out more about Cathy and her books at www.cathygillenthacker.com, and you can write her c/o Harlequin Books, 300 East 42nd Street, New York, NY 10017.

Books by Cathy Gillen Thacker

HARLEQUIN AMERICAN ROMANCE

HARLEQUIN BOOKS

Who's Who
in the Deveraux Family

Tom Deveraux—The head of the family and CEO of the Deveraux shipping empire that has been handed down through the generations.

Grace Deveraux—Estranged from Tom for years, but back in town—after a personal tragedy—for some much-needed family support.

Chase Deveraux—The eldest son, and the biggest playboy in the greater Charleston area.

Mitch Deveraux—A chip off the old block and about to double the size of the family business via a business/marriage arrangement.

Dr. Gabe Deveraux—The "Goodest" Samaritan around. Any damsels in distress in need of the good doctor's assistance…?

Amy Deveraux—The baby sister. She's determined to reunite her parents.

Winnifred Deveraux Smith—Tom's widowed sister. The social doyenne of Charleston, she's determined never to marry. That's not what she has in mind for her niece and nephews, though.

Herry Bowles—The butler. Distinguished, indispensable and devoted to his boss, Winnifred.

Eleanor Deveraux—The Deveraux ancestor with whom the legacy of ill-fated love began.

Chapter One

Chase Deveraux knew from the moment he got the summons to the Deveraux family's Meeting Street mansion that it was going to be hard as all get-out to hold on to his temper. And that was never truer than when he walked in the front door and saw his woman-stealing brother Gabe standing next to the fireplace in the drawing room.

Gabe looked at Chase with his typical do-gooding innocence and said, "I can explain."

"I'll just bet you can," Chase replied sarcastically, his temper escalating all the more. There were times he was glad he and his three younger siblings had all decided to settle permanently in Charleston, South Carolina, along with their father, instead of taking jobs at various places around the country as many of their friends had done. This wasn't one of them.

He glared at his baby brother and pushed the words through his teeth. "The only problem is, I don't want to hear it. Not after what I saw at noon today."

"Maggie called me." Gabe heeded Chase's low warning tone. "It was a medical emergency."

Chase lifted a brow in raging disbelief as he moved across the brilliant-blue carpet, embossed with gold stars. "One that required mouth-to-mouth resuscitation, no doubt."

"I'd have thought you would have had more sense than that," Mitch, the second oldest son, scolded their baby brother as he took off the jacket of his pearl-gray business suit and jerked loose the knot of his austere silver tie. "Seeing Maggie Callaway is bad enough, after what she did to this family two years ago." Mitch grimaced in disbelief as he spoke for the group assembled. "But kissing her? In front of Chase? That's low, Gabe!"

Amy, the peacemaker, as well as the youngest of the family, stepped into the breach. Maybe it was because she and Gabe were closest in age, but she was always quick to rise to Gabe's defense. "Isn't it possible that you misunderstood what you saw, Chase?" she asked anxiously as she fussed with the pink roses set out in crystal vases around the house. "After all, if it was a medical emergency—if Maggie fainted or something—maybe Gabe was just doing what had to be done. He is a doctor, for heaven's sake!"

"Is that what happened?" Chase asked as he turned back to the increasingly guilty-looking Gabe.

The old bitterness and betrayal cut him like a knife as he pushed away the mental image of Gabe and Maggie staring deep into each other's eyes, even while Maggie had still been engaged to marry *Chase!* Not that it had mattered. In the end Gabe hadn't suffered any qualms about betraying his brother. Then or now. Family loyalty was something Gabe apparently just didn't have. "Did Maggie call you out to her beach house because she was feeling faint?"

Gabe said nothing.

More furious than ever, Chase continued, "Let me guess what happened next. You rushed over. She answered the door—swooned at the sight of you. And then you hauled her into your arms and laid a big one on her. All in the name of medical science, of course."

Looking guiltier and all the more uncomfortable, Gabe dragged a palm across his jaw. "She didn't faint." It was his turn to push the words through his teeth as he moved toward the floor-length sash windows that graced both ends of the elegantly appointed room.

"Then what happened?" Mitch sank down on a Duncan Phyfe chair, which was covered in the same brilliant-blue-and-gold-star pattern as the carpet.

"I can't really say," Gabe replied with a reluctant shrug. "Beyond the fact that Maggie called me and asked me to meet her at her place, pronto."

"For…?" Amy probed curiously, when Gabe didn't go on.

"That's confidential," Gabe replied stiffly as he moved beneath the portrait of Revolutionary War hero General Marshall Deveraux.

"I'll just bet it is." Deciding he'd had enough of trying to play it cool, Chase went straight for his father's whiskey and poured himself a shot.

Gabe met Chase at the bar. He helped himself to a club soda over ice. "Look, if you must know, she was talking to me about a medical matter."

Chase knew his brother had worked hard to perfect his bedside manner during med school and residency, but this was ridiculous. "Is that how you minister to all your patients?" Chase asked, deliberately goading Gabe. "By kissing them?"

"She's not my patient," Gabe said hotly. "All I was doing was listening to her and offering advice."

Chase would have liked to believe it was just that innocent. Just as he would have liked to believe that Maggie's feelings for his brother had been platonic, from the get-go. Unfortunately that wasn't true and he knew it. The minute Maggie had laid eyes on Gabe, her engagement to Chase might as well have been history. And that was a public humiliation Chase still found very hard to take, regardless of the fact that his feelings for Maggie, whatever they had been, had long ago faded to obscurity.

"Then what were you doing giving her mouth-to-mouth?" Chase demanded, trying to push the image of the two standing on Maggie's doorstep, wrapped in each other's arms, out of his mind. If that wasn't a sign of some ongoing clandestine rendezvous, he didn't know what was!

"That kiss you saw today just happened," Gabe countered hotly. "We didn't plan it. Any more than you planned to be driving by at the exact second I was saying goodbye to her."

"I see. It was an accident. Just like your stealing Maggie away from me just two days before our wedding and then dumping her the moment her wedding to me was officially off was an accident."

Gabe glared at Chase in frustration. "I couldn't get involved with her after what had happened to our family!"

Chase snorted derisively as he choked down a swallow of fine Southern whiskey. "Too bad you couldn't have decided that before you wrecked my wedding plans," he fumed.

"If anyone wrecked your wedding plans, Chase, it was you."

Chase set his glass down with a thud. He turned away from the sideboard and asked ever so slowly, "What did you say?"

Gabe's eyes gleamed with temper. "You heard me. If you'd just paid one-tenth the attention to Maggie that you pay to your work at the magazine…"

Chase flushed. Was it his fault Maggie had led him to think she was a low-maintenance woman, when the truth was she was anything but? "If she'd wanted me to sit around listening to her all the time, I would have done so!" Or at least he would have tried, Chase amended silently, knowing as well as everyone else in the room that he had a very low tolerance for chitchat.

"A woman shouldn't have to tell you that," Gabe shot back, looking even more peeved.

That wasn't Chase's experience with the fairer sex. The women he dated couldn't have cared less about scintillating conversation—they wanted passion and sex. Period. Besides, he'd never been able to read a woman's mind the way Gabe could.

"Now listen," Amy broke in, anxiously wringing her hands, "Chase and Maggie's breakup was probably bound to happen, anyway. Because of the Deveraux family legacy—"

Chase and Gabe groaned in unison. "Not that again," Chase said, shooting an exasperated look at his little sister.

"Amy might have a point," Mitch said with extreme civility. He looked at Chase sternly, acting more like the older brother. "If you and Maggie had managed to marry and live happily ever after, you would have been the first Deveraux to do so in three generations."

Chase scowled. "Our failed betrothal has nothing to do with the curse put on our great-aunt Eleanor."

"Tell that to everyone who's had their love life wrecked for no reason in the past sixty years," Amy countered. "And then tell me the curse hasn't carried over to the next Deveraux generation!"

Gabe glared at Chase, even as he addressed his remarks to his two calmer siblings. He downed the rest of his club soda in a single gulp. "I still say I had nothing to do with the breakup. If Chase and Maggie had been meant to marry, they would have. Curse or no curse. And nothing I said or did or didn't say or do would have stopped them from tying the knot."

"You just keep telling yourself that," Chase said sarcastically. He'd had some miserable days in his life, but he'd never been more hurt and humiliated than he was the day Maggie had walked out on him and their wedding. For he'd known then that it wasn't just his divorced parents or brother Mitch— who was also divorced—who were unable to find and keep wedded bliss. People just didn't stay together in this day and age. They didn't find happiness in the act of permanently joining their life with another's. Hell, nowadays they were lucky if they could even make it to the altar and say "I do." And learning that lesson the hard way had made him stop trying to find the "happily ever after." Instead, it made him look to the immediate present for his happiness, and no further.

"Moreover," Amy continued passionately as she stuck her hands in the front pockets of her pastel coveralls, which were embroidered with the name of her decorating business, "Chase needs to get over the way Maggie walked out on him and be glad she came to her senses before they entered into a marriage that most likely would have ended in divorce, anyway. And most important of all, he needs to stop trying to seek revenge for Maggie's actions on the whole female population!''

"And how am I doing that?" Chase demanded furiously, incensed to find Amy—who could usually be counted on to soothe the wounded egos of all three of her brothers—scolding him, too. It wasn't as if he promised women anything but what he could give them, which was today!

Amy gave him a droll look as she explained, "You do that by turning women into objects in your magazine and trying to nail every female in Charleston."

Chase shook his head in exasperation, knowing that the very well-paid models for *Modern Man* never complained about how beautiful they looked in the pages of his magazine. "Actually, that's old news. I've moved on—" Chase quipped, knowing even as he spoke it wasn't entirely false "—to the entire East Coast."

"That's not funny, Chase." Amy scowled.

"It's not supposed to be," Chase retorted bluntly, using this—and every other opportunity that came his way—to shamelessly plug the premise of the notoriously lighthearted and controversy-inspiring magazine he had created just for guys. "Women are here on this earth for one reason and one reason only. To make guys happy.'' And as far as he was concerned, guys were only there to make women happy. It was pretending otherwise, in his opinion, that made people so darn miserable.

''And that tally includes dear old Maggie,'' Chase continued, deliberately ignoring the warning glare Gabe gave him. ''Which is undoubtedly the reason Gabe rushed out to the beach house.'' Chase turned to his brother and proceeded to hit Gabe where he knew it would hurt the most—Gabe's legendary sense of duty. ''Maggie was lonely. She was desperate.'' *And like the rest of us mortals, in urgent need of some happiness to call her own.* ''So she dialed the emotional equivalent of 911, and Gabe here, ever the good Samaritan, rushed right out to administer the much-needed and -wanted, obligatory mercy—''

Chase never had the chance to finish his sentence. But then, he thought, with a certain grim satisfaction as Gabe's fist came flying up to meet him, he'd known for certain he never would.

BRIDGETT OWENS parked her Mercedes convertible at the rear of the Deveraux mansion and headed in the servants' entrance. She paused just long enough to kiss her mother's flushed cheek and ask, ''What's the emergency?''

Theresa Owens grabbed a floral-print apron from the drawer and slipped it on over her uniform—a plain navy-blue dress with a white collar. Tying her apron behind her as she moved, Theresa headed swiftly for the ancient subzero refrigerator in the corner. Quickly she pulled out a package of fresh crabmeat and another of cream cheese. "Grace is coming home." Theresa checked her recipe and collected milk and horseradish from the fridge and an onion from the mesh basket on the counter. "Tom went to the airport to get her. All the children are here. And I'm short-staffed."

"Where is everyone else?" Bridgett asked. Tom Deveraux had a chauffeur and a gardener, in addition to her mother, his full-time cook and housekeeper.

Theresa brushed auburn tendrils off her face with the back of her hand. "It's their day off."

"Mom, you should have a day off," Bridgett said, wishing her mother would listen to her and give up working as a domestic. Especially now that it was no longer necessary. Theresa could retire and live with Bridgett and never have to worry about money or putting a roof over their heads again.

Theresa frowned as she measured ingredients into the casserole dish and stirred them together briskly. "Then who would cook for Tom?"

"Maybe he could order takeout?" Bridgett suggested as her mother slid the crabmeat dip into the oven to bake. "Or eat at a restaurant."

Theresa wiped her hands, then restored order to the bun on the top of her head. "I have all the time off I need whenever I need it."

Bridgett sighed, knowing she was about as likely to talk her mother into taking early retirement at fifty as she was to get her to change her hairstyle or stop wearing the "uniform" that Tom and Grace Deveraux had both told her years ago she did not have to wear. "Except you never take any time off," Bridgett reminded her mother gently.

"Honey, I don't have time to argue with you." Theresa went back to the refrigerator for salad fixings. "I'm trying to put together a dinner party for six on thirty minutes' notice. And Tom said it was crucial that everything be very nice."

Bridgett zeroed in on the concern in her mother's voice, even as she did what she had done for years, as the daughter of a Deveraux domestic—pitched in to lend a hand. "Did something happen?" Bridgett asked as she rolled up her sleeves and helped her mother make a dinner salad on the fly.

"I'm not sure." Her expression increasingly worried, Theresa got out the food processor and set it on the counter. "But he said Grace might be upset when she gets here and he wanted all the children to be in attendance so they could talk to them together."

A feeling of foreboding came over Bridgett as she watched her mother fit the slicing disk into the machine. Bridgett hadn't seen much of Grace Deveraux since Grace had gone to New York City to host the *Rise and Shine, America!* morning news program fifteen years ago, but she cared about her nonetheless. She cared about all the Deveraux, just as her mother did. "Grace isn't ill, is she?"

Theresa shrugged. "I'm not sure Tom knows what this is all about, either. But you know how it's been between the two of them since they divorced."

"They can hardly stand to be in the same room with each other."

"So if Grace called Tom and asked him to pick her up at the airport and bring her here, of all places…"

To the home the two of them had shared in happier times.

"It must be bad," Bridgett concluded, reading her mother's mind.

Theresa nodded.

And it was then, as she looked at her mother's face, that Bridgett realized the real reason her mother had called her. Not because she needed help preparing dinner or carrying a tray of canapés. But because she needed moral support in dealing with whatever the fallout of Grace and Tom's news. Theresa might insist on reminding herself daily in a million little ways that there was a huge class difference between the Owenses and the family Theresa had worked for since before Bridgett was born, but Theresa and Bridgett both loved all the Deveraux like family nevertheless. "How is Chase and everyone taking this?" Bridgett asked, knowing that Chase was likely to have a tough time with any calamity involving his parents. Maybe it was because he was the oldest, but he had taken his parents' divorce thirteen years ago especially hard.

"I'm not sure," Theresa said, jumping and grimacing at the big thud and shouting from the front of the house. Then the sound of glass breaking.

"Apparently," Bridgett said, answering her own question, "not so well."

There was another crash, even louder. Then the sound of Amy screaming.

"Oh, dear." Theresa's hand flew to her chest and she got a panicked look on her face.

"Sounds like another fight." One of many, both before and after Tom and Grace's divorce. Bridgett sighed. She put up a hand before her mother could exit the kitchen. "I'll go, Mom." She had experience breaking up fights. Why should this one be any different?

"DAMMIT, GABE, I don't want to hurt you." Ignoring the pain across his shoulder, where he'd caught the edge of the mantel, Chase staggered to his feet. He pressed one hand to the corner of his mouth, which seemed to be bleeding, and held Gabe at bay with the other palm upraised between them. "So back off!"

Gabe shook his head, his expression angry, intense, and continued coming, fists knotted at his side. "Not until you take back what you said about Maggie," he stormed.

Chase smirked, not above taunting a self-righteous Gabe. "Right. Like you plan to take back sucking face with her?"

"That does it!" Gabe leaped over the back of the sofa, grabbed Chase by the shirt and swung again, his fist arcing straight for Chase's jaw.

Chase ducked the blow and countered with a punch to Gabe's gut. As he expected, it didn't do much damage. Gabe had been ready for him, muscles tensed. Just as Chase was ready for the tumble over the upholstered Duncan Phyfe chair to the floor. Gabe landed on top of him, but not for long. Chase forced him over onto his back. He grabbed his brother by the front of his shirt, still seeing red. For the life of him, Chase didn't understand why Gabe continued to defend—and apparently desire— the woman who had come as close to two-timing Chase as any woman ever would. Especially when Gabe had to know how hurt and humiliated Chase had been, both by the events and all the sordid speculation that had followed. Not that it had been any easier for Gabe and Maggie. Both their squeaky-clean reputations had been forever tarnished, too. And for what? It wasn't as if the two of them had found any happiness, either. "Gonna give up now?" Chase demanded in frustration, wishing they could put this ugly episode behind them before it further destroyed their family.

"Not on your life." Gabe scowled back, looking ready to do even more damage.

And that was when it happened. A shrill whistle

split the air and two spectacular female legs glided into view. Sexy knees peeked out beneath a short silk skirt. His glance then took in slim sexy calves, trim feminine ankles and delicate feet clad in a pair of strappy sandals. Chase knew those legs. He knew her fragrance. And he especially knew that voice. It belonged to one of the most sought-after financial advisers in Charleston, South Carolina.

"One more punch, Chase Deveraux," Bridgett Owens said sweetly, "and you're going to be dealing with me."

THE FIRST THING Chase thought was that Bridgett Owens hadn't changed since he had last seen her. Unless it was to get even better-looking than she already was. Her long auburn hair had been all one length when she'd gone off on her phenomenally successful book tour three months ago. That soft-as-silk hair still fell several inches past her shoulders, but now it was layered in long sexy strands that framed her pretty oval face. She'd done something different to her eyes, too. He couldn't say what it was exactly, though he figured it had something to do with her makeup, because her bittersweet-chocolate eyes had never looked so dark, mysterious or long-lashed. She was wearing a different color of lipstick, too. It made her lips look even more luscious against her wide, white orthodontics-perfect smile.

She was also dressing a little differently.

Maybe it was because she also ran a private financial-counseling service out of her home and hence felt the need to present a serious, businesslike image to the public that she'd worn suits that were so tailored and austere it was almost ridiculous. Today, however, she was wearing a silky pencil-slim skirt that was so soft and creamy it looked like it was made of raspberry-swirl ice cream. With it she wore a figure-hugging tank top in the palest of pinks and a matching cardigan sweater. The overall effect was sophisticated, feminine and sexy. Too sexy for Chase's comfort.

"Honestly," Bridgett continued, seeming to scold Chase a lot more than Gabe, "aren't you two a little old for such nonsense?"

Chase scowled. The last thing he wanted—from anyone—was advice on how to handle the restoration of his pride. "This is none of your business," he fumed, still holding tight to Gabe's shirt.

"The heck it's not!" Bridgett charged closer, inundating Chase with the intoxicating fragrance of her perfume. "When it's gonna be my mother explaining to your parents what happened to all the priceless furniture here!"

"No explanation needed," came a deep male voice from somewhere behind them.

Every head turned. There in the portal stood Tom Deveraux, dressed in a dark business suit, pale-blue shirt and conservative tie. Coming in right behind him was Chase's mother, Grace. As the two of them stood frozen, looking at their two brawling sons, it was almost like going back in time for Chase—before his mother had moved to New York City. Before the estrangement between his mother and father, which neither he nor his siblings really understood to this day. To the time when they had been, for whatever it was worth, a family that was united, even in times of strife. Nowadays it seemed that all they had left was the strife. And the heartache of a once-loving family that had fallen apart.

"I suppose we don't even have to ask what was the reason for this," Grace said wearily, touching a hand to her short and fluffy white-blond hair.

Chase immediately noted the strain lines around his mom's mouth, the shadows beneath her blue eyes, and his heart went out to her. Something had happened, he thought, and it was bad enough to bring his dad to her side again.

"If the two of you are fighting like this, Maggie Callaway has to have something to do with it," Tom surmised frankly, clearly disappointed in both of them.

Neither Gabe nor Chase said anything.

Bridgett offered Chase her hand. Though hardly ready—or really even willing—to end the brawl with his woman-stealing brother, Chase took the assistance Bridgett offered. And, to his mounting discomfort, found his old pal Bridgett's manicured hand just as delicate in shape, strong in grip and silky soft as it looked.

Tom continued shaking his head at everyone in the room, then settled on Mitch and Amy. "You couldn't have stopped this before they broke half the vases in the room?" he asked them.

Amy made a face and brushed her long hair, a dark brown like Tom's, from her eyes. "It's sort of a long story, Dad."

Mitch shrugged his broad shoulders. "Amy and I figured they were going to come to blows again, no matter what. Better it happen here. Where they're unlikely to get arrested or otherwise bring dishonor to the Deveraux name."

Tom looked at Chase and Gabe. His lips thinned in disapproval as he demanded, "What do you two have to say for yourselves?"

"Not a thing," Chase muttered, resenting being questioned like this at his age, even if he and Gabe did deserve it.

Gabe grimaced, looking at that moment like anything but the good Samaritan he was. "Me, neither."

Tom turned to Bridgett. "At least you were trying to break it up."

Bridgett smiled at Tom respectfully. "Someone had to. And since I have…I think I should excuse myself."

"No reason for that," Grace said, putting up a staying hand before Bridgett could so much as take a step out of the drawing room. "You're family, Bridgett, you know that. Besides, I have something to tell you all,'' Grace added, just as Theresa came into the room, a silver serving tray of hot crabmeat dip and crackers in hand. "Sit down, everyone." Grace waited until one and all complied, including Theresa, before she continued reluctantly, "I wanted you to hear this from me before it hits the airwaves." Grace paused, took a deep breath. "I've been fired."

Chapter Two

Chase stared at his mother, barely able to believe what he was hearing. "What do you mean, you've been fired!"

"They can't fire you!" Mitch cried, incensed, as the entire Deveraux family closed rank around Grace. "You're the a.m. Sweetheart!"

Looking even more upset than their mother, Amy argued emotionally, "The American public loves you! They said so at last year's Favorite Celebrity awards!"

Grace sighed and shook her head. "It doesn't matter."

"Since when?" Chase asked, incredulous, unable to understand how his mother could remain so resigned in the face of such a professional catastrophe. For the past fifteen years, her whole world had revolved around that job. She had given up her life in Charleston, sacrificed her marriage and what little happy family life they'd had, at that point, for that job. "Amy's right, Mom. The morning news shows sink or swim on the personality of their cohosts."

Grace sat down, looking unbearably weary. Her skin was pale against her cheerful yellow tunic and matching trousers. "The show's ratings have been sinking for some time now."

Gabe picked up an overturned chair and set it to rights. He looked their mother square in the eye. "You're sure you can't do anything to change the network's decision?"

Again, Grace shook her head. "It's not just me," she said softly. "They're replacing my cohost, too. And going with a younger couple."

The family gave a collective sigh as Tom went over to the bar and fixed a tall glass of diet soda and ice. He brought it back to Grace and sat down next to her.

"When is all this going to happen?" Chase asked. He caught Bridgett's gaze and saw she was just as concerned about his mother as he was. That was no surprise. He knew Bridgett loved his mother, too.

Grace cupped the glass in both her hands and ducked her head. "The network is going to announce my replacement later today. It'll probably be on the evening news tonight. It may make the Internet before then."

"You're not going to hold a press conference?" Mitch, ever the businessman, asked.

Grace shook her head. "I'm letting my publicist

handle it. We crafted a statement together before I left New York. She'll release it.''

"And then what?" Gabe asked. "Will you be going back to finish up?"

"Surely the network is going to give you a big send-off," Amy said.

Grace sipped her soda. "The network wanted to make a big deal about my leaving, but I told them I didn't want it. Those things are always maudlin. I'd rather viewers remember me just as I was this morning, when I taped my last show. Besides, it's not the last time I'll ever be on television. My agent is already fielding offers. They began coming in last month when there were rumors a change was going to be made."

Silence fell. Chase noted with no small amount of admiration that his mother seemed to be handling this catastrophe better than the rest of them. "So what are you going to do now?" he asked casually after a moment.

"Your mother is going to be staying here at the mansion," Tom said. "I'll be staying at a hotel."

Chase wasn't surprised. That had been the case ever since his parents' divorce. Whenever his mother came to Charleston, she stayed at the family mansion, and his father moved—temporarily—to the Mills House Hotel. It was the only way his mother could get any privacy, she was so well-known. She was besieged by autograph hounds if she checked into a hotel. And staying at the mansion made it easier for her to see all four of her children.

"Now, if you don't mind," Grace said, suddenly looking as if she was going to burst into tears, after all, "it's been a very long day and I think I'll go upstairs and lie down. That is, if you boys think you can stop fighting long enough to give us all some peace."

"They had better—" Tom Deveraux cast a warning look at his sons "—or they aren't half the men I thought they were."

"WELL, I GUESS he told us," Chase murmured after his father and mother had disappeared up the wide sweeping staircase.

Bridget looked at Chase. "It's not as if you didn't deserve it," she said, clearly exasperated. "You and Gabe are far too old to be rolling around on the floor."

"I'll certainly second that!" Theresa Owens fumed, like the second mother she was to them all. "Chase, you're bleeding. And Gabe, you need some ice on that eye."

"You take care of Gabe. I'll take care of Chase," Bridgett told her mother. Before Chase could reply, Bridgett had him by the sleeve of his loose fitting linen shirt and was tugging him toward the powder room tucked beneath the stairs. She shut the door behind them, pushed him down on the closed commode and began rummaging through the medicine cabinet for supplies.

"Just like old times, huh?" Chase said. Glad Bridgett had volunteered to act as his nurse, but sorry she had witnessed his humiliation and juvenile behavior, he began unbuttoning his ripped shirt to get a look at the stinging skin underneath.

Bridgett set the antiseptic, antibiotic cream and bandages on the rim of the pedestal sink. She turned back to him, pushed up her cardigan sleeves and prepared to get to work. "You haven't punched out Gabe since the wedding that wasn't, have you?"

"No." Chase peeled off his shirt and stared at the nasty-looking scrape that ran from his left shoulder to midchest and down his arm. He was pretty sure it had happened when he slammed into the mantel and slid to the floor. "Although maybe I should have," Chase added as he touched his lip and found that it, too, was still bleeding, just a little bit. "Gabe still doesn't seem to have learned his lesson about stealing someone else's woman." Chase grimaced as he checked out a rug burn beneath his right elbow.

"He stole another of your girlfriends?" Bridgett frowned at the scrape on his forearm.

Chase scowled, recalling. "I saw him and Maggie at her beach house a few hours ago. They were kissing."

Bridgett wet a sterile pad with warm water,

doused it liberally with soap, and began washing the scraped skin. "You and Maggie are back together?"

"Hell, no!" Chase clamped his teeth together. Damn, that stung! And damned if Bridgett didn't seem to enjoy making it sting, too!

"Then why does it matter if Gabe kisses her?" Bridgett added more soap and moved on to his shoulder.

Chase tried not to think about how good it felt to have her hands moving across his skin in such a gentle, womanly way. Bridgett was and had always been his friend, not an object of lust. "Because she was my woman and I was there first!" Chase hissed again as Bridgett dampened another sterile pad and rinsed away the soap on his skin.

Bridgett shrugged. "If that's your only objection, she was right not to marry you."

Chase shot her a look. He didn't care if the two of them had been as telepathic as twins since the moment they were born. He didn't like the censure in Bridgett's low tone. "What do you mean by that?" he demanded, turning toward her.

"I mean," Bridgett enunciated as if speaking to a total dunce, "I understand your not wanting him to kiss her if you were in love with her, but if you're not—"

"I'm not," Chase interrupted firmly.

"Then it shouldn't matter to you. Period."

"Well, it does." Chase bristled under her watchful gaze.

"Why?" Bridgett dabbed antibiotic cream across his shoulder.

"Because it's like pouring salt in a wound," Chase explained in frustration, wishing she would hurry up and get this over with.

"One that obviously has yet to heal," Bridgett countered, moving close enough to Chase that he could see the barest hint of cleavage revealed by the décolletage of her form-fitting sweater set. He swallowed around the knowledge that Bridgett's breasts were fuller and rounder than he had ever realized. Or wanted to realize.

"I'm over her," Chase said, struggling to keep his mind on Maggie, instead of Bridgett and what her closeness, her sheer femininity, were doing to him.

"Just not over the humiliation of being dumped by her," Bridget guessed, apparently oblivious to the discomfort she was causing him.

Chase shifted his weight to relieve the unexpected pressure at the front of his khaki beach shorts. "You got it."

Bridgett unrolled sterile gauze across his shoulder. "Well, then, I suggest you get over it," she advised, her warm hands brushing across his even warmer skin as she taped the bandage into place.

"And why would that be?" Chase asked, feeling as if he was going to explode if he had to sit there for one more second.

Bridgett looked at him sternly. "Because if Gabe

was kissing her today, Chase, that can mean only one thing. Gabe still has the hots for Maggie. Even after all this time. And he doesn't care who knows it.''

Chase vaulted to his feet, grabbed his shirt and shrugged it on. "I'm tired of talking about me and my unconscionable behavior. Let's talk about you and yours," he said, leaning back against the closed bathroom door.

Bridgett squared her slender shoulders and shot him a stern look. "I don't behave unconscionably."

Chase quirked a brow, wondering if she had missed seeing him as much as he had missed seeing her. And how was it the two of them had grown so far apart, anyway? Was it just because they were older with different personal and career agendas to pursue? Or was there more to it than that? "You used to get into trouble right along with me," he said softly, thinking about the fun the two of them had had during their childhood and teen years. It had only been later, after college, that they'd begun to drift apart. To the point that these days they rarely saw each other at all. And then, only by chance.

The picture of efficiency, Bridgett put the first-aid kit back in the medicine cabinet. "I've grown up," she told him plainly.

Too much, Chase thought, wondering when it was, exactly, that Bridgett had gotten so serious. "So I see." he shot her a teasing leer, meant to make her laugh.

"Cut it out, Chase," she ordered. Frowning, she gathered up the paper bandage wrappers and excess bits of tape and tossed them into the trash.

Chase could see he had offended her, when that was the last thing he'd wanted. "You used to have a sense of humor."

Bridgett shrugged and continued to avoid looking at him. "I used to be immature."

"And now you're not."

"No." Bridgett lifted her head and looked at him coolly. "I'm not."

Silence fell between them. Chase knew she was ready to leave the intimate confines of the guest bath, but he didn't want to let her go. Not yet. Not with the mood between them so unexpectedly tense and distant. He folded his arms in front of him and asked seriously, "How was your book tour? I assume you just got back."

Finally the sun broke out across her face. "Last night," Bridgett confirmed happily. "And the experience was wonderful, if grueling, and very satisfying, economically and personally. Just the way every three-month book tour should be."

Chase found himself warming to the deep satisfaction he saw on her face. He had always wanted the very best for her. Always known she would get it. "Did you really cover every region across the country?"

Bridgett nodded, the depth of her devotion to her work apparent. "And I helped more women than I can say,'' she confided, leaning back against the sink.

Maybe it was because he had grown up wealthy as sin and knew firsthand how little real joy a hefty bank account could bring a person, but it bothered Chase to know that Bridgett valued money more than just about anything these days. She used to treasure more than that. She used to treasure her friends—especially him. ''Just what this world needs.'' Chase sighed, ready to goad her back to sanity, if need be. ''Even more women who think money is the route to happiness.''

Bridgett scowled at the sarcastic note in his low tone. ''It is.'' She crossed her arms beneath her breasts defiantly.

Chase kept his eyes on hers. ''If you say so.'' He inclined his head indifferently.

The fire in Bridgett's eyes sparked all the hotter. ''Don't belittle what I do for a living, Chase.''

''Why not?'' Chase pushed away from the closed door and stood straight, legs braced apart, once again. ''You certainly belittle what I do,'' he reminded her as he narrowed the distance between them to just a few inches.

Bridgett straightened, too. ''That's because your magazine—''

''*Modern Man,*'' Chase helpfully supplied the publication's name, in case she'd forgotten.

"—does nothing but teach guys how to get what they want from women!"

"What's wrong with that?" Chase demanded. Clueless for as long as he could remember about what women really wanted or needed in this life, he had started his magazine as a way of collecting data from other men, about what worked and what didn't with the women in their lives. As far as Chase was concerned, he was providing a public service, making both men and women a little happier, while doing his part to tamp down the battle of the sexes and reduce the number of unhappy relationships overall.

"I'll tell you what's wrong with that." Bridgett planted her hands on her hips. "It makes guys think that women are 'a problem to be handled' and that there is something fundamentally wrong with marriage."

"There *is* something fundamentally wrong with marriage," Chase shot back flatly, not about to sugarcoat his opinion on the subject on her account. "Or hadn't you noticed the soaring divorce rate in this country?"

Bridgett released a long slow breath. She looked as if she was fighting for patience. "Lately the divorce rate has actually been going down. No thanks to you!"

Chase brought his brows together in consternation. "You don't know that," he argued back. He was tired of taking the blame for things that were way beyond his control. "Maybe I'm the one to credit for that." He knew for a fact, from reader mail, that there were a lot of guys who had really appreciated his series on how to get their women not to just tolerate, but love the sports they followed. The same went for his series on cooking in, instead of eating out.

Bridgett rolled her eyes. She stared at him, making no effort to hide her exasperation. "And how do you figure that?" she asked drolly.

"Because," Chase said, thinking how much he had always enjoyed a spirited argument with Bridgett and how much he had missed having them with her since she'd been away, "I also run articles that convince guys not to get married when they're not ready."

Bridgett's eyes turned even stormier. And worse, looked hurt. "Exactly."

Too late Chase realized he had hit a real sore point with Bridgett. The fact that her own parents had never married, even when Theresa Owens had gotten pregnant. "I'm sorry," he said swiftly, seriously. "I know your, uh—"

"Illegitimacy?" she provided when he seemed unable to blurt it out.

"—is a real sticking point with you," Chase continued, with some difficulty. It was, he knew, probably the biggest hurt of her childhood, though she rarely talked about it.

Bridgett waved him off, already done talking

about it, and ready to move on. "I just think you're doing a disservice to men with that whole marriage-isn't-really-all-that-necessary attitude you and your magazine perpetuate."

"Yeah, well, I think I'm helping my readers," Chase said stubbornly. He was making them see that marriage was a serious step. And if they weren't serious about a lifetime commitment, or the women they were chasing weren't serious about the same, marriage was not the path to take. He certainly didn't want them to end up a public laughingstock, the way he had, when his bride had ditched him just days before they were to marry.

"Whatever." Bridgett tugged the sleeves of her elegant silk-and-cotton cardigan down to cover her wrists. "It doesn't matter to me."

Like hell it didn't, Chase thought, studying the wealth of emotion on her face.

"I'm late, anyway," Bridgett continued.

"For what?" Chase asked curiously. And that was when he saw it. The big fat emerald ring.

Chapter Three

Bridgett thought she was past the third degree when it came to Chase and her beaux. Apparently not. He still felt—wrongly so—that he had the right to comment on the men she chose to date. Not to mention the gifts they might have or have not chosen to give her.

"What," Chase demanded, his handsome features sharpening in disapproval as he looked down at the emerald ring glittering on the ring finger of her right hand, "is that?"

Bridgett had an idea what he was going to say. She didn't want to hear it. Deliberately misunderstanding where he was trying to go with this, she lifted her shoulders in an indifferent shrug. "I can't buy myself a ring?"

Chase's sexy slate-blue eyes narrowed even more. He took a step closer and said, very low, "I know you, Bridgett. You invest in real estate, growth stocks, a car that will go a couple hundred thousand miles before it quits. You don't spend thousands of your hard-earned cash on baubles. Someone gave you that very pricey emerald-and-platinum ring.''

Someone he apparently already didn't like, even though he had yet to find out who it was. ''So what if it was a gift?'' Bridgett shot back just as contentiously. Expensive as the ring was, she knew that to a man like Martin, it was just like penny change. Martin never did anything in a small or inconsequential way. When they dined out, it was at the very best restaurants. They drank the rarest, most expensive wines. He didn't just send her roses. He gave her vases of the most exquisite orchids or lilies. Once, he'd flown her to Europe for the weekend, simply because he wanted her to see Paris in the springtime. Initially, of course, she'd tried to discourage such lavish gifts. Now she knew that was just the way Martin and everyone else in his family lived.

Chase braced a hand on the wall just beside her head. ''I want to know who gave you that ring.''

Bridgett refused to let him intimidate her with his I'm-in-charge-here body language. Honestly, she didn't know how Chase did it! She had been back in Charleston less than twenty-four hours and already Chase—the bad boy of the Deveraux clan—was already under her skin. Big time.

She angled her chin at him defiantly ''I don't have to answer you.''

"Darn it, Bridgett. You know how much I care about you."

Cared, Bridgett thought, but didn't love. Would never love. At least not in the way she had once wanted desperately for Chase to love her. Now she knew better, of course. Chase might have once considered her his very best buddy and partner in mischief, but when it had come to dating, he had always chosen others. At first she had thought—wrongly— it was just because he was romancing women from his own social class. That theory had been blown out of the water when he became engaged to Maggie Callaway, who was from the same working class background as Bridgett. Then she had known that social status was not the reason Chase didn't pursue her. He simply wasn't attracted to her. Not in that way. So she had put any lingering hope of a romance between them aside and kept her distance from Chase as much as possible. She had known then what she had to remind herself of now. Chase protected her and watched out for her in a familial sort of way. There was nothing the least bit romantic in his feelings toward her—and never would be.

Silence fell between them. "Your mother didn't tell me you were engaged," Chase said finally when she didn't respond to him.

"That's because I'm not yet," Bridgett explained with a great deal more patience than she felt.

He dropped his arm, stepped back until he was once again leaning against the opposite wall of the first-floor powder room, his six-foot-two-inch frame dwarfing her own five-foot-seven one a little less. "But you're close," Chase asserted unhappily, still studying her face.

"I think we're definitely headed that way. Yes."

Abruptly Chase looked as if he had received a sucker punch to the gut. Again Bridgett warned herself not to take his reaction personally. Chase was probably just suffering the pangs any "brother" would have about seeing his "sister" married off.

"Who's the lucky guy?" Chase asked finally in a rusty-sounding voice.

Bridgett tried not to notice how handsome Chase looked in the soft lighting of the room. After all, it wasn't as if she wasn't used to his stunning good looks. She had grown up looking into those long-lashed, slate-blue eyes of his and knew full well they were the color of the ocean on a stormy day. She had committed to heart the rugged planes of his face, the square jaw, the high cheekbones and wickedly sexy smile. Okay, maybe his shoulders did look a little broader and stronger, his abdomen a little flatter, since the last time she had seen him. Maybe he was a little more tan and rough around the edges. But the ensemble of pleated khaki shorts, loose-fitting short-sleeved shirt and sneakers was the same. Chase wanted people to see him as a slacker when she knew full well he was anything but. Deep down he was as ambitious and determined to succeed in business as she was, if not more so.

"The guy?" Chase prodded again when Bridgett failed to answer his query. "The ring giver does have a name, doesn't he?"

Bridgett flushed. "Martin Morganstern."

Chase shook his head and looked all the more disappointed and distressed. "Not the art-gallery guy over on King Street," he said, groaning.

"One and the same," Bridgett confirmed, unable to help the haughty edge that came into her voice. "And you needn't speak of him with such derision."

Chase rolled his eyes. "Man, Bridgett! That guy is old enough to be your father!"

Bridgett forced a droll smile as she allowed, "Only if I were sired when he was thirteen."

"Which makes him…?"

Bridgett pushed aside her own lingering uneasiness that there was something just not right about her and Martin, despite the fact that on paper, anyway, when it came to all the relevant facts, they looked very good as a couple. "He's forty-five."

"To your thirty-two." Chase blew out a gusty breath and slammed his hands on his hips. "The guy's too old for you. Way too old."

Bridgett shrugged. She didn't know why, exactly, but Chase was making her want to punch him. "You're welcome to your opinion," she told him icily. "Fortunately," she said as she tried to step past him once again, "I don't have to abide by it."

Chase smiled as if he had an ace up his sleeve

and once again stepped to block her way. "What does your mother think about that ring?" he asked smugly.

Another alarm bell went off in Bridgett's head. Ignoring the probing nature of Chase's gaze, she said stiffly, "She hasn't noticed it yet." She'd been too busy in the kitchen.

Chase immediately had an "Aha!" look on his face.

Bridgett grimaced all the more. "I was about to show her when you and Gabe started brawling."

Chase smirked. "Likely story."

Not for the first time in her life, Bridgett wished Chase didn't know her so well. "I'll do it later," she said.

Chase ran a hand along the light stubble on his jaw and continued to regard her smugly. "I think you're stalling."

Bridgett squared her shoulders as if for battle. "I am not."

Chase lifted his dark brow in silent dissension. "Your mom won't approve of you accepting such a lavish gift from him," he predicted matter-of-factly.

Unfortunately Bridgett was pretty sure Chase was right about that, since to date Theresa hadn't approved of much of anything Martin had done.

"In fact," Chase predicted, leaning even closer, "I bet she doesn't like you dating Martin any more than I do, does she?"

"Fortunately for me," Bridgett parried, ignoring the warmth emanating from Chase's tall strong body, "it's not up to my mother whom I should or should not spend time with."

Chase's brows drew together like twin thunderclouds. "You should listen to her, Bridgett. Your mother has always had a lot of sense."

"In most matters." Bridgett felt her hackles go up as she delineated precisely, "Not this."

"You need to give that ring back, Bridgett."

"Really." Taking exception to the tone of his voice, Bridgett folded her arms beneath her breasts contentiously and glared at him. "And why would that be?"

Because that ring is the kind of gift a man gives to announce a woman is his. And his alone. And I just can't see you with a smooth talker like Morganstern, Chase thought. Aware she was waiting for an answer and fuming while she did so, Chase did his best to conjure up an answer. "Because you're too young to get that serious about someone," he said finally.

"I'm thirty-two," Bridgett shot back, temper sparking her beautiful brown eyes. "If I want to have a family of my own—"

"You've got plenty of time for that."

Again she looked down her nose at him, as if he just didn't get it. "I'm ready to get married and settle down now," she explained as if to a moron.

Chase frowned, and unable to help himself,

blurted out in frustration, "At least find someone who can make you happy while you do it!"

Bridgett propped her hands on her hips. "What makes you think Martin won't make me happy?"

Because I just know, Chase thought, uneasiness sifting through him. Aware how lame that would sound, he remained silent.

Bridgett stared at him as if she had never seen him before and had no clue who he was. "Like I said, I've got to go." She ducked around behind him and exited the powder room without another word.

CHASE WAS DISAPPOINTED he hadn't been able to make Bridgett see what a mistake she was making even dating Mr. Wrong. But that didn't mean he was giving up. He figured it would take time—and persistence—to make Bridgett see the error of her ways. But he figured she'd be grateful to him in the end. He didn't want her suffering the way he had when he'd been betrothed to the wrong person.

In the meantime he needed to check on his mother. He found Grace upstairs in the guest room where she always stayed. She had changed out of her travel clothes and into a slim apple-green dress that only seemed to emphasize her recent weight loss. The strain lines on her face seemed all the more pronounced in the late-afternoon sunlight streaming in through the windows. "Are you going to be okay?" He didn't know why, but she seemed more vulnerable now than when she had first arrived and told them she'd been fired. He wasn't used to his take-charge, kick-butt mother being weak.

"Of course I'll be all right," Grace said in the firm parental voice she had used on him and his siblings. She looked at him sternly. "I don't want you worrying about me."

"Can't help it." Chase sauntered into the bedroom and shut the door behind him, so they could talk privately. "In the first place, I'm the oldest son."

"Which does not make you responsible for me."

Maybe that would've been true had there been someone else—like a husband around all the time—to protect her. But there wasn't. "Even so, in your place, I'd be reeling," Chase told her frankly.

Grace opened the first of several suitcases with a beleaguered sigh. "I've suffered setbacks before, Chase."

Chase knew she had. First and foremost among them had been her legal separation from his father, a year after she had moved to New York City to work on *Rise and Shine, America!* Another year after that, there'd been the finalization of the divorce. None of which Chase understood to this day. Oh, he knew marriages didn't last anymore. And maybe they never should have lasted for decades even in years past, when that was the norm. Most of the married couples he knew did not seem all that happy once the wedding rings were on their fingers, the shackles around their ankles.

"Plus, I work in television," Grace continued, as she took out a stack of clothes and put them neatly in a dresser drawer. "Being hired and fired is all part of the routine business cycle."

"It still must hurt," Chase persisted, taking a seat on the ivory chaise in the corner.

Just as the divorce had hurt. Not that Grace and Tom had ever let their kids see them quarrel. It had been their strict policy not to let their four children be privy to anything going on in their marriage, especially anything bad. The idea, of course, had been to protect Chase and his siblings from any unpleasantness. And so all their kids had thought everything was fine when it was not, and had ended up feeling baffled and distressed when Grace and Tom—for no reason any of their children could fathom—suddenly stopped speaking to each other and began living separate lives. Chase had often wondered what the breaking point had been. Had one of them been unfaithful or done something equally unforgivable? And if so, why? Was the love between a man and a woman something that could just end without warning or reason? Frustratingly these weren't the kinds of questions his parents fielded. All he knew for certain was, after they'd split, the anger and bitterness between Grace and Tom had been fierce and unrelenting. And that tension had gotten worse, before it had ever gotten better. These days, of course, the two were able to be cordial to each other—at least on the surface. But deep down, Chase still felt there were problems that remained unresolved to this day. Divorce or no divorce.

"I admit my pride is wounded," Grace said in a way that reminded Chase that this was the first time his mother had been fired from a job. Previously whenever Grace had left a television show, it was to take a better position at another show.

Grace took out several pairs of shoes and carried them to the shelf in the closet. "It hurts having the failure of the show blamed on me and my cohost. But that's just the way it is in the business." Grace returned to her suitcase for her toiletry bag. "Whoever is out in front takes the credit or the blame, and in this case it was blame that needed to be apportioned out to appease the sponsors."

Restless, Chase got up to help. "Something better will come along. Before you know it, you'll be back in New York on another network," he assured his mother as he unzipped the first of her two garment bags.

Grace smiled ruefully as she lifted out the clothes already on hangers and carried them to the closet. "I'm not sure I want to work in early-morning television again. Getting up at three-thirty every morning did not do much for my social life. I was going to bed for the night when everyone I knew was just getting off work for the day."

"Then something that airs later in the day,"

Chase persisted, pushing away the disturbing thought of his mother wanting to keep company with any men besides his father. It had been bad enough occasionally coming face-to-face with his father when he was squiring other, usually much younger, women around. Now he'd probably be seeing his mother going out on dates, too. "An afternoon talk show, maybe," Chase suggested.

Grace made a face as she set out her hairbrushes and combs on the old-fashioned vanity. "Right now that sounds like even more of a grind. No. What I want to do right now is spend more time with you and your brothers and sister, Chase. I've missed that."

Chase warmed at the idea of being able to see and talk to his mother whenever he wanted again and still live and work in the city he had grown up in and come to love like no other. "We've missed you, too, Mom." More than she would ever know. It was their dirty little secret, but without Grace around, the Deveraux did not seem like much of a family. Not the way they once had been, anyway.

Grace enveloped Chase in a warm hug. "And besides, I've always wanted to learn how to cook."

"I THOUGHT YOU'D BE happy for me," Bridgett told her mother emotionally. She had just shown her the emerald ring Martin had given her after picking her up at the airport and taking her to dinner the evening before. "I thought you wanted me to be happy."

And frankly she was hurt that her mother wasn't more enthusiastic about the serious turn her relationship with Martin was about to take.

"I do want you to be happy," Theresa explained gently. "Which is why I want you to spend time with someone whose background is similar to yours."

"Not to mention," a deep male voice said from the doorway, "someone your own age."

Theresa beamed at Chase the way she always did whenever he entered a room. "See, he agrees with me," Theresa said as Chase kissed her cheek.

"Chase just doesn't want to see anyone get serious," Bridgett said, more irritated than ever to have Chase putting his two cents in about her personal life. She stopped folding napkins for her mother long enough to glare at Chase. "Chase does not believe in monogamy, never mind marriage."

Chase plucked a carrot from the salad Theresa was making. He shrugged his broad shoulders without apology as he turned back to Bridgett. "I certainly don't believe you should yoke yourself to some hoity-toity art dealer."

"Hoity-toity?" Bridgett echoed in amazement, unable to believe Chase had actually used such a term.

"Haughty, arrogant, condescending." Chase pulled up a stool and joined them at the butcher block, where they were preparing dinner.

"I know what it means," Bridgett countered irritably, wishing Chase would just go away. She put the last of the fan-shaped napkins into a basket for her mother. "I write for a living, too, you know."

"Martin's old money, darling," Theresa warned. "Very old money. And you know what they always say…"

"The rich are different," Bridgett repeated wearily. She had heard that old saw from her mother a thousand times.

"Not all of us." Chase helped himself to a tomato wedge. "Some of us old money fellas are down to earth. Just not ol' Martin Morganstern of the Morganstern Gallery of Charleston. Martin is as blue-blooded and luxury-loving as they come."

Bridgett found herself defending her soon-to-be fiancé hotly. "He's very nice."

Chase raised a dissenting brow as he added salt to the tomato wedge.

Theresa sighed as she continued to whip up a vinegar-and-oil dressing. "All men are nice when they're trying to…to…"

"Get into my bed?" Bridgett guessed, saying what her mother seemed unable to articulate.

Theresa flushed with embarrassment but did not back down as she poured dressing on the salad and tossed it. "You're the daughter of a domestic servant, Bridgett. You may want to forget that. But ten to one, in the end, Martin Morganstern and his very old and very proper family won't."

REALIZING IF SHE DIDN'T get a move on, she was going to be late, Bridgett said goodbye to her mother and headed out the back door. To her dismay, Chase followed her. "Your mom is right," he said as he shadowed Bridgett out to her Mercedes. "What you have is new money. To a guy like Martin Morganstern, there's one heck of a difference. To a guy like me, well, cash is cash."

Bridgett unlocked her car and tossed her purse inside. "Thank you ever so much for enlightening me." Hot air poured out of the sedan's interior through the open door.

"I don't care if you have any money or not," Chase continued while Bridgett waited for her car to cool down before she got in. "I am and will always be your friend, regardless of your financial circumstances." Chase folded his arms on the top of the door and continued to regard her with a cheeky seriousness that really got under her skin. "Can you really say the same about Martin Morganstern?"

Realizing she would be too hot with her cardigan on, Bridgett slipped it off, and tossed it on the seat beside her purse. She ignored the way Chase's gaze slid over her bare arms and shoulders. "You've been listening to my mother for too long!"

Chase grabbed her wrist before she could slide in, his fingers warm on her skin. "Your mother is just trying to keep you from getting hurt," he said seriously.

"And what's your excuse for butting into my

life?'' Bridgett turned away from the stormy gray-blue of his eyes and put up a hand to stop any further diatribes. "Don't answer. I really don't want to know."

Afraid she would lose it if they said anything else to each other on the subject, she started her car and drove off.

MARTIN WAS WAITING for Bridgett in the Barbados Room in the Mills House Hotel. He was wearing a sage-green suit with a tie and white shirt. His black hair was neatly brushed away from his handsome face, his gray eyes alert and interested. As always, he looked thrilled to see her approaching him. Just being with Martin made her feel calm inside, not all fired up and agitated the way she was when she was with Chase Deveraux.

As she neared, he stood and helped her with her chair. "I ordered you a glass of wine."

Bridgett smiled gratefully, appreciating his gentlemanly manners. "Thank you."

"What's wrong?" Martin studied her silently. His glance fell to her right hand, before returning to her eyes. "Don't tell me. Your mother thinks you shouldn't have accepted the ring I gave you."

Bridgett didn't have the heart to tell Martin how upset her mother had been about the gift and what it might mean when he had been so excited about giving it to her. So she said only, "My mother's very old-fashioned when it comes to a lot of things.''

Martin frowned. ''You should have let me come with you when you went to see her today.''

That would have only made things worse, Bridgett thought, because there was no telling what her plain-spoken mother would have said to upset a quiet cultured man like Martin. ''It'll be fine,'' Bridgett insisted, glancing at the menu.

Martin studied her. ''I hope so. I really want your mother to like me. That's rather hard to manage when she never spends any time with me.''

Bridgett swallowed. She had tried to get her mother to have an open mind about her relationship with Martin—to no avail. Her mother thought people should get married only if they were wildly in love and of similar backgrounds. She and Martin flunked that litmus test. Their backgrounds were as different as night and day, and as for their feelings for each other, well, those were more of a tranquil nature. Steady and reliable. Without the ups and downs of passion. What no one seemed to understand, Bridgett thought, was that this was what she wanted. A relationship that was as safe and dependable as municipal bonds. She didn't want to be worried about being abandoned by the man she loved, the way her own mother had. Nor did she want to worry about getting divorced, the way Tom and Grace had. It was so much better, she thought, to enter into a lifelong relationship with someone with a cool head and a sensible attitude.

Martin continued to watch Bridgett, waiting.

"My mother is going to need a little time," Bridgett said finally, thinking that a guaranteed low-yield investment was better than the ups and downs of a high-risk annuity any day.

"I have been patient, darling," Martin said gently, covering her hand with his.

Bridgett swallowed and tried not to think how heavy and almost uncomfortable the emerald-and-platinum ring felt on her right hand. She looked into Martin's eyes. "I know you have," she said softly.

"I waited for you throughout the long months of your book tour."

And he had never complained about her absence, Bridgett thought in her soon-to-be fiancé's defense. Not once.

"But my patience," Martin continued, "is almost gone."

HOURS LATER, Bridgett's mind was still reeling with all Martin had demanded of her as he walked her to the front door of her newly acquired "single house" in the historic district of Charleston. Like all town homes of the early 1800s, the single-pile redbrick Georgian had been turned sideways on the narrow city lot. A two-story piazza, or covered porch, had been built along the length of the building to provide outdoor living space for each floor, as well as shade on the windowed facade. On the first floor the street-front room was her office, where she worked on her books and advised clients on financial matters. The single room behind it was an eat-in kitchen. On the second floor, she had a combination master bedroom and bath at the front of the house and at the rear a cozy sitting room, where she relaxed, read, watched television and entertained. It was small but perfect, and as soon as Bridgett had purchased it, she had known she had really made it. No longer was she merely the daughter of the housekeeper of a well-heeled Charleston family. Now she was one of the elite that kept the city humming.

"You'll call me in the morning to let me know what you've decided?" Martin said as he ever so tenderly increased his grip on her hand.

Bridgett nodded as she looked into his eyes. "Absolutely."

"Sleep well, my precious." Martin brushed his lips across her temple. He turned and headed down the sidewalk to the car at the curb. Bridgett waited, enjoying the splendor of the cool spring evening, until he'd driven away before she turned to let herself inside. And that was when she saw him, relaxing in the shadows, of her first-floor piazza.

Chapter Four

"My precious!" Chase echoed. "Who says something like that? Oh, right." He snapped his fingers. "Someone from the *previous* generation."

Bridgett told herself she was not in the least bit glad to see him as she unlocked her front door. "What are you doing here?" She tried to behave as if she wasn't perturbed by the fact that Chase had been not just waiting for her to come home from her date, but had declined to make his presence known right away, spying on her and Martin, as well.

"Isn't it obvious?" Chase strolled around to join her and followed her into the house. "I came to talk to you."

Bridgett shut the door behind them. "It's after midnight, Chase."

"I know." Chase made himself at home on the red damask settee.

Bridgett noted he was still in the casual clothes he'd had on earlier, with one exception. He'd taken off the shirt he'd torn in the brawl with Gabe and put on a plain blue oxford-cloth dress shirt that looked as though it might have belonged to his dad. He'd left the shirttails out and rolled the sleeves to his elbow. "You changed your shirt," she said.

"Had to." He sat back amiably and propped an ankle on his knee. "Dinner with the folks."

Deciding the room was much too cozy with only one lamp burning, Bridgett walked around the room and turned on a few more lights. "How'd that go?"

Chase's eyes turned serious as she came back to join him in the small sitting area of her home office. "It was exceptionally quiet. Gabe got called back to the hospital halfway through. Amy was her usual worried self. And Mitch seemed preoccupied— something to do with the family shipping business. I wasn't really paying attention."

"What about your parents?"

"They were pretty quiet, too. I had the feeling they wanted to spend some time alone, talking about Mom's situation, I'm sure. They were just going through the motions of a family dinner to reassure us everything would still be okay, despite the very public firing."

"Once a parent, always a parent, I suppose."

"I guess." Chase surveyed her midnight-blue silk chiffon sheath, with the handkerchief hem and matching chiffon shawl. He regarded her in a way that reminded her just how well he knew her.

"What are you doing out so late on a weeknight, anyway? Don't you have to work tomorrow?"

Knowing he was right—normally she would be in bed a lot earlier on a weeknight so she could be up bright and early the next morning to write or meet with the clients she was advising on financial matters—Bridgett sat down in a straight-backed chair opposite from him. "I'm taking a few weeks off before I start my next project," she said. "And I have no client appointments scheduled for the next week, either."

"Good. Glad to hear it." Chase leaned forward earnestly, hands clasped between his spread knees. "Because I need your help. Professionally speaking."

"I'm not writing anything for *Modern Man*," she told him flatly.

"Sure now?" Chase flashed her a sexy grin. "We could use a woman's perspective on money matters. You wouldn't even have to write anything. We'd conduct it interview-style. And I'll put it all together in an article about you and your success."

Bridgett knew that where Chase was concerned, nothing was this simple. If he wanted to do something, it was because he knew his readers would benefit in ways specifically aligned with his way of thinking. She had to think for a minute to figure out how Chase would probably spin it. "So you can tell your readers how to get women to do what they want in a financial sense,'' Bridgett guessed. *While still avoiding marriage like the plague.*

Chase flattened a palm against his rock-solid chest and regarded her with mock hurt. ''You sound like you've been listening to my critics.''

''I've been reading your magazine,'' Bridgett said.

''And...?''

''If you really want to know, I think you're so off base in your assessment of the current battle between the sexes, it's ridiculous.''

''Come on, Bridgett.'' Chase gave her a look that begged for understanding. ''Most of the stuff you're referring to is meant solely to amuse.''

''You and I know that.'' Bridgett crossed her legs demurely at the ankle and continued to regard Chase seriously. ''I'm not sure most of the male population under thirty does. I think they take all your advice about how to thrive as bachelors very seriously even the stuff that is clearly over the top.''

Chase regarded her with lazy indifference. ''Maybe that's because my readers don't want the wife, the house and the two kids in the suburbs. When they do start wanting that stuff, they stop reading *Modern Man* and move on to whatever it is married guys with kids read.''

Chase had always been fun-loving and reckless to a fault, but in the wake of his own broken engagement and his parents' divorce, he had also become a lot bitterer than she figured even he realized, and her heart went out to him. She looked at him and said with as much gentleness as she could muster, "You're going to find another woman, Chase."

Chase scowled as if the last thing he wanted was Bridgett's pity. His jaw set as he vaulted from the sofa and paced her home office. "I didn't come for advice on my love life."

"I figured that," Bridgett retorted. It didn't mean she wouldn't give it. Particularly when he'd been so free to comment on *her* love life.

"But there are a couple of matters I do want to discuss." Chase shoved his hands in the front pockets of his khaki shorts.

"Okay."

His manner abruptly serious, he continued, "First I want you to talk to my mother for me. About her finances. I want to make sure she's all set, despite this firing."

Bridgett hedged, aware Chase was once again treading where he shouldn't. "I'm sure your mother already has excellent financial advisers."

His eyebrows assumed a troubled arch. "I'm not so sure about that. She's never had much interest in financial matters. To tell the truth, she made so much money with *Rise and Shine, America!* and has been so slow about spending it that she never felt it mattered. Now, with a sudden drastic reduction in her income, it may matter a lot. You've had a great deal of experience in getting women who don't want to deal with their finances to face the music. I just thought if the two of us took my mother to lunch tomorrow, we could talk about your work and how successful you've been for yourself and your clients in your private financial-counseling service. And then see if we can get my mother to ask for your advice or at least accept it and read one of your books. That last one was particularly on the money, in my opinion.''

"You've been reading my books?'' Bridgett tried not to make anything of the fact that he was as up on her work as she was on his.

Chase shrugged. "I wanted to see if you knew what you were talking about,'' he admitted with partially disguised pride. "You do.''

Despite her annoyance with him, his respect meant a lot to her. As did the fact that he had come to her, instead of one of his own financial advisers, with this request. "I'd be happy to help you, Chase.''

"Good.'' He breathed a sigh of relief.

"But I have to warn you,'' Bridgett continued, "I think you better be prepared to be very subtle with your mother. If you come on like gangbusters, in the wake of the humiliation she has already suffered in being fired…''

Chase lifted a palm as if being sworn in. "I'll be the soul of discretion, I promise.''

Bridgett moved gracefully to her feet, knowing she really needed to get him out of her house before the mood between them became too intimate. She didn't want to feel this close to him, as if they were still and always would be the very best of friends. Not when she was getting ready to say yes to a marriage proposal from another man. "Well, if that's all..." she said politely, dropping her chiffon shawl on the chair.

"Actually it's not." Chase blocked her way to the door. Ignoring the impatient expression on her face, he said, "I want to know if there's any real passion between you and Marvin."

Leave it to Chase to get right back to that, Bridgett thought on a beleaguered sigh. Leave it to him to make her have to explain. "His name is Martin, Chase. Not Marvin. And we have passion," Bridgett declared, hating the defensive note that had crept back into her voice.

"Oh, yeah, I could see that." Chase rolled his eyes and shook his head as he recounted, "The guy brought you home and didn't even give you a proper good-night kiss! If that's what it's like now, what is it going to be like for the two of you after you get married and things really cool off?"

A flush climbed from Bridgett's neck to her face. She hated Chase's ability to follow the track of her thoughts—and concerns—so easily. "Martin respects me," she countered testily, pushing her own nagging doubts about what she was doing aside.

"You mean he treats you like a porcelain figurine he doesn't want to damage," Chase corrected.

"You're not going to be happy sitting on a shelf in some rich man's house, Bridgett."

Bridgett marched past him and grabbed the door handle. "Get out." She forced the words through her teeth.

Chase caught up with her and flattened his hand against the wood next to her head, holding the door shut. "Not until I've had my say," he said.

The air was coming in and out of Bridgett's lungs with difficulty.

"I don't want to see you hurt," he said next.

Tears of frustration welled in Bridgett's eyes. "*You're* hurting me."

"What can I say?" Chase countered, his expression as stern and unrelenting as the words he tossed at her. "Sometimes the truth knocks you on your butt. Only, I care about you too much to stand by while you throw your life away."

Bridgett wished that was true. When they were growing up, she would have given anything for Chase to notice her and want to protect her like this. But he hadn't. He had treated her like his best pal— and that was all. Eventually she'd had to face the fact that he didn't desire her in the way she desired him and never would. She'd been devastated. So devastated, in fact, that she had done her level best to avoid being alone with him like this ever since. They'd been together in groups, but never absolutely alone. Never like this.

"Why are you looking at me like that?" he asked softly, brushing the hair from her face.

Because I want you to see me as a woman, Bridgett thought, desire welling up inside her with the force of a tidal wave. *Because just once I want you to haul me into your arms and kiss* me *like there's no tomorrow.* Not about to tell him that, however, she angled her chin stubbornly, glared at him for a long pulse-throbbing moment, then turned away and said, "Because I want you to stop interfering in my life and telling me what to do."

"Is that right?" Chase challenged. He caught her by the shoulder and brought her gently but determinedly back around to face him.

"It's absolutely positively right!" Bridgett shot right back.

And the next thing she knew, she was in Chase's arms and he was lowering his mouth to hers. Their lips met in an explosion of softness and heat, pleasure and need. Bridgett murmured a quiet "Oh!" of surprise and another helpless whisper of breath. His tongue touched hers, lightly at first, then with growing ardor, his passion igniting her own. Longing shifted through her, more powerful and wonderful than anything she had ever felt—or dared imagine. She whimpered again, more helplessly still, against the sensual pressure of his lips. "Bridgett," Chase whispered as his arms brought her closer still, until her breasts were pressed against the hardness of his chest and their bodies were almost one. Lower still, she felt the flatness of his abs and stomach, the hard demanding evidence of his desire, the strength in the arms around her. She melted against him, threading her hands through his hair, completely caught up in the liquid mating of their lips and tongues. She had always known if he kissed her, it would be like this.

Chase hadn't come over there to kiss her, hadn't ever let himself consider the possibility of the two of them being anything but friends. But now that they were kissing, he found he couldn't stop the feelings pouring out of him. Bridgett felt so right in his arms. So sweet and giving. She made him want to be lost in her, in this. But even as he thought it, he knew he couldn't allow their embrace to go any farther. Not before he got a few things straight, anyway.

Reluctantly he lifted his head, stepped back. He swore silently at the regret and confusion already in Bridgett's dark-brown eyes. He could tell she was already wishing they hadn't crossed this bridge in their relationship. And that disappointed him more than he could say.

"What was that all about?" Bridgett demanded, glaring at him as if the searing embrace was all his fault and she hadn't kissed him back at all.

Angry that she had shifted the blame to him, Chase shrugged. And as always, when he felt his happiness or status quo threatened, he fell back on his customary devil-may-care attitude. "I'll be damned if I know," he said.

Chapter Five

"You can't just come in here and kiss me like that and then tell me you don't know why you did it!" Bridgett stormed. Just then her phone rang.

The problem was, Chase thought, as Bridgett's phone continued ringing, he did know why he did it. He'd been seeing red ever since he had seen the ring on her right hand earlier that day and known she was about to make the mistake of her life. That feeling had only intensified when he had seen Martin leave her at her door without so much as a real good-night kiss. Bridgett deserved more, he thought furiously. A helluva lot more. But unable to tell her that—when clearly all she wanted him for was a pal and a sort of unofficial brother—he shrugged. "I wanted to show you what you'd be missing if you hitched yourself to that old geezer."

Bridgett gave him a look that revved up his motor even more, then asked with so much feigned sweetness he wanted to haul her into his arms and kiss her all over again, "Meaning, if I don't marry him, you'll keep supplying me with passionate kisses?"

"Do you want me to keep supplying you with kisses?" Chase asked, as Bridgett's prerecorded message on her answering machine finally ended. A beep sounded, signaling it was time for the caller to leave a message, and then a familiar female voice filled the room.

"Bridgett, darling, it's happened again!" Chase's aunt, Winnifred Deveraux-Smith said. "I've seen Eleanor! And I can't find anyone to help me witness it—Chase, Amy, Gabe, Mitch, Grace and Tom are all out! So call or come over if you can!" The machine clicked as the message ended.

Chase groaned and slapped the heel of his hand against his forehead. "Not again," he grumbled. "Two mentions of that ghost in one day are all I can take." First Amy had suggested that the curse put on Eleanor—and by association the whole family—was the real reason his engagement to Maggie had ended. And now Aunt Winnie—the only member of the family who had ever actually encountered the ghost of the long-since-departed Eleanor—had experienced another ghostly encounter.

Bridgett plucked her evening bag and keys off the table. "Well, I'm going over there." She wrapped her shawl around her shoulders.

Chase frowned. "Not by yourself, you're not."

Bridgett glided past him as he held the door for

her. "Now why would you want to go over there, Chase? You don't believe in ghosts."

"Exactly." Chase waited for Bridgett to lock up, then escorted her to his Jeep. "Someone has to talk some sense into Aunt Winnifred and put all this nonsense to rest before you and Amy and everyone else in the family starts believing it, too!"

Bridgett watched Chase circle around the front of the vehicle and climb into the driver's side. "There have been some unexplained phenomena. Besides, it doesn't matter if you or I or Amy or anyone else believes in this ghost. Your aunt Winnifred does. And as long as she thinks there's a curse on the members of your family, preventing anyone and everyone from living happily ever after, she will never remarry."

Chase frowned as he drove the short distance to his aunt's residence on East Battery. The three-story pink-stucco mansion overlooked the eastern side of the Charleston peninsula and had a magnificent view of the bay. The Greek-revival mansion also had a piazza on all three stories, as well as a parapet on the roof that bore the family coat of arms. When his aunt gave big parties, as she was inclined to do on a regular basis, people spilled out onto the porches, the lawn and sometimes even the roof and had a wonderful time.

Chase noted from the way the place was lit up that it looked like his aunt had thrown a party that very night. He led Bridgett through the front gate of the tall black wrought-iron fence that surrounded the house on all sides and up the elegantly land-scaped walk to the front door.

"Aunt Winnie might never remarry, anyway. Mom and Dad both said she was devastated when her husband was killed in that training mission on his first year of active duty with the military." It had been nearly twenty-seven years, and Winnie showed no signs of being completely over her loss.

Bridgett exchanged concerned looks with Chase. "Thank goodness Winnifred has Harry."

Chase knew exactly what Bridgett meant. Winnifred's butler was more than just a family employee, he was Winnifred's right hand. There'd been a bit of a scandal when Aunt Winnie hired Harry, of course. Her husband had barely been dead a year, and the very British Harry was far too handsome and close to Winnifred in age for people not to won-der if it was wise for them both to be living—more or less alone most of the time—under the same roof. But the gossip had faded over time when Harry had remained Winnifred's trusted loyal servant and clos-est confidante and nothing more.

Harry answered the door. His pale-blond hair was slicked away from his face, and he was wearing black tie, tails and gloves. Looking resplendent in a shimmering evening gown, the fifty-year-old Winni-fred was right behind him. "Oh, Chase, thank good-ness you're here, too!"

"Why?" Chase asked as he followed Bridgett inside. He noted that Winnifred's cheeks were awfully pink.

"Because it was you Eleanor was warning me about!"

"What'd she do?" Chase quipped, becoming more amused by the minute. "Repeatedly call my name?" If he didn't know better, he'd think his aunt was matchmaking.

"Of course not," Winnifred said as she lifted the skirt of her party gown and made her way up the sweeping circular staircase to the second-floor sitting room. "Eleanor made a lot of noise in the attic, which was what drew me up there, and when I got there, she was sitting on the trunk that contains all the toys you used to play with when you were a child. So I know it's you she's concerned about this time."

Chase looked beyond Winnifred to Harry. "How much champagne has she had this evening, anyway?"

"Not enough to imagine that," Winnifred said sternly, looking at Chase in a way that left no doubt in anyone's mind she was sober as a rock. "If you don't believe me, you can—" She stopped midsentence as they heard light rustling sounds on the floor above. "You see!" Winnifred cried joyously. "There she goes again. Calling us up there!" Winnifred rushed toward the attic door. "Hang on, Eleanor, we're coming!" she shouted. Harry was right behind her, flashlight in hand.

"Did you see the ghost, too?" Chase asked Harry as he tucked Bridgett's hand in his and pulled her along beside him.

Harry shook his head as Winnifred yanked open the door to the attic and all four of them were assaulted with a blast of remarkably frigid air. "I was downstairs paying the caterers," Harry said.

Winnifred hit the light switch as she ascended the stairs to the third floor. Noticing Bridgett was shivering in her thin evening dress, Chase tugged her close and wrapped an arm around her shoulders.

Chase wasn't surprised to see the attic still remained just the way he recalled it. Big steamer trunks of family belongings fought for space with the odd piece of furniture and a dressmaker's dummy from years past. "Show me where you saw Eleanor," Chase said.

Frowning—probably because there was no ghostly apparition anywhere in sight and all the noise had stopped, too—Winnifred picked her way across the crowded attic floor and stopped just short of an antique oval mirror. "Right over there," she pointed to the trunk just in front of the mirror. "I saw her sitting right there when I rushed up the stairs."

Maybe because Eleanor Deveraux was considered a "friendly" ghost, Winnifred wasn't the least bit afraid of the apparition she'd seen.

Chase frowned as he tried to figure out a logical explanation for what his aunt had seen. "Are you sure you didn't just catch sight of yourself in the mirror?'' he said. ''If you were excited about seeing Eleanor again…'' Sightings of the ghost were infrequent at best, usually tied to some family romantic calamity. In this case, Chase felt, the calamity would have had nothing to do with him or with Bridgett. In this case, the calamity would have been his mother returning to Charleston—the city where her ex-husband/Winnifred's brother still lived—and Winnifred's ever-present hope that Grace and Tom would finally patch up their differences and reconcile so that at least someone in the Devearaux family would defy the legacy and be happily married at long last.

''I think I can tell the difference between gold-and-white silk brocade—which was what Eleanor was wearing this evening—and my own red-silk evening gown, Chase. Furthermore—''

Feeling a lecture he did not want to hear coming on, Chase interrupted and held up a staying palm. ''Look,'' he said with a great deal more patience than he really felt, ''I didn't mean to imply—''

Without warning, the lights in the attic flickered and went out, leaving them in total darkness.

''See?'' Winnifred cried. Harry switched on his flashlight and swung the illuminating beam around. ''You've ticked her off, Chase.''

''It's probably just a fuse,'' Chase said.

Bridgett tensed. Able to feel her trembling, Chase tightened his arm around her. Harry handed Chase the flashlight. "I'm going down to the root cellar to check the fuse box. If there's nothing wrong there, I'll bring up some lightbulbs. Maybe they just all need to be replaced."

"I'll go with you," Winnifred said, trembling, too. She pointed at Chase and Bridget and commanded, "You stay here and wait for the ghost."

Chase focused the flashlight on the path Harry and Winnifred needed to take to make it safely down the attic stairs. When they were gone, he turned back to Bridgett. "Sorry about all this," he said, although in truth he wasn't sorry at all. This latest disaster-in-the-making was giving him an excuse to be close to Bridgett again, physically, as well as emotionally.

"You can't help what your aunt believes." Bridgett shivered and snuggled more closely in the protective curve of his arm.

Chase drank in the fragrance of her perfume. "The question is, what do you believe?" he asked softly, studying the pretty contours of her upturned face. "Do you think there's a ghost up here?"

Another gust of chill air descended on them, causing Bridgett to shiver all the harder.

"I don't know what to think," Bridgett whispered as nervously as if they'd been overheard. "Intellectually, of course, I know there are no such things as ghosts." She wrapped her arm around Chase's waist. "And yet, people all over Charleston have claimed to have seen any number of ghosts over the years. We've had books written about them."

Chase grinned. "Not to mention created some very lucrative tourist traps," he added in amusement.

"And then there's Winnifred. If she says she saw Eleanor here tonight—" Bridgett broke off at the rustling sound in the darkness behind them, close to the trunk and the antique mirror.

"Maybe it's just a mouse," Chase said.

Bridgett moaned at the thought of that and wrapped her other arm around Chase's waist. Chase would have liked to stay that way forever, with Bridgett clinging to him. Unfortunately they had a mystery that needed to be solved. Determined to see what had been making the racket, Chase extricated Bridgett from his arms. Then he positioned himself in front of her and ever so carefully, ever so slowly, leaned forward, until he could just about see over the trunk to the floor between trunk and mirror. Bridgett was right behind him, hanging on to his waist for dear life, her body shielded completely by his.

Like him, barely daring to breathe, she poked her head around, stood on tiptoe and ventured a look. And that was when it happened, when something small and furry leaped up and flew right past her face.

Bridgett's scream was loud enough to wake the dead. Chase bit down on a thousand curses, too vile to mutter in a lady's presence. And then, whatever it was, headed straight back for them.

Bridgett screamed again and wrapped herself even more tightly around Chase—arms, legs, every possible inch of her was pressed tightly, desperately against every inch of the front of him. "Do something!" she cried as Chase dropped the flashlight, and the furry thing zoomed right past their faces. Bridgett, who wasn't about to let go of Chase even when he bent down to get his flashlight, screamed again before all went quiet.

Trembling, near tears, Bridgett looked up at Chase. He wanted nothing more than to kiss her again. But knowing that would have to wait until he'd gotten her safely out of the attic and away from whatever it was they had disturbed, Chase turned the beam toward the stairs. "Do you think you can walk?" She was so frightened she seemed damn near frozen in his arms.

She nodded and kept clinging. "Just get me out of here," she gasped.

Chase hugged her close and complied. As soon as they reached the bottom of the stairs, the lights in the attic came back on. Chase left them on in hopes of quieting or scaring away whatever was still up there and led a still-shaking Bridgett out of the attic.

Harry and Aunt Winnifred met up with them on the landing between the first and second floors. Winnifred took one look at Bridgett's pale face and the way she was clinging to Chase and said, "You saw Eleanor's ghost, too, didn't you?"

"WE ONLY WISH," Chase said as he ushered Bridgett into the closest sitting room, the second-floor library, and settled her on the antique cream sofa in front of the fireplace. "I'm sorry to tell you, Aunt Winnie," he continued as he gathered up a cashmere throw and slid it around Bridgett. "But you've got some kind of vermin up there."

Winnifred's jaw dropped in stunned amazement.

"I don't think it was a bat, but whatever it was," Chase continued, "it was definitely flying."

Winnifred pressed a hand to her throat. "Are you serious?"

Chase nodded. "You're going to need to call Clyde's Critter Removal Services first thing in the morning and get him out here to take care of whatever is up there."

"I guess that means you didn't see Eleanor?" Winnifred looked disappointed as Harry returned with a snifter of brandy. He poured four glasses, then passed them out, one by one.

"Not even a glimmer of our dear family ghost," Chase confirmed. "Sorry."

"I wonder, though," Aunt Winnifred said thoughtfully, "if it was all some kind of sign…?"

"What are you getting at?" Chase asked impatiently.

"I thought Eleanor had appeared tonight because

she was worried about you. But maybe that's not it at all.'' Winnifred looked at Chase and Bridgett thoughtfully. "Maybe what Eleanor really wants is for you and Bridgett to be together," she said.

Chapter Six

Bridgett stared at Winnifred, wondering how her evening could get any more bizarre. "You can't be serious," she said.

"Oh, I am. Quite. Eleanor, you see, never does anything without a darn good reason. And if she got you and Chase here tonight, then she must want you two to be together."

Bridgett looked at Chase helplessly. He knew as well as she did that Chase's being at her place when Winnifred's call came was pure accident. His desire to tag along with her was also a whim that had nothing to do with the wishes of any ghost!

Chase held up his hands in surrender. "Don't ask me for explanations," he said, clearly amused. "I never claimed to know anything about ghosts, never mind be privy to their secret agendas and wishes."

"I've always thought the two of you belonged together, anyway," Winnifred continued as she settled into a chair across from Harry and sipped her brandy. "Isn't that right, Harry? From the time I saw Bridgett and Chase playing together as kids, I said, 'Those two are going to grow up and marry each other one day.'''

"Only one problem with that, Winnifred," Bridgett said, tongue in cheek. "I am currently dating someone else."

Chase braced an arm along the back of the sofa and leaned over her. "Exclusively?" Chase cut in, the flexed muscles of his thigh nudging the softer ones of hers. "Or casually?"

Bridgett turned her gaze away from Chase's and moved slightly forward so they were no longer touching. "I don't know what you mean," she said.

Chase caught her wrist before she could stand. Not about to let her off easily, he regarded her with a probing smile. "Have you promised not to date anyone else?"

Trying not to notice how her wrist was tingling beneath the warmth of his grip, Bridgett drew the cashmere throw more closely around her shoulders. "There's been no formal agreement between us." Chase arched his brow skeptically, prompting Bridgett to add, "I mean, we're not in high school, for goodness' sake."

Chase released his hold on her and sat back against the cushions of the sofa. "So you've been dating others?"

"No. I've been too busy doing interviews and personal appearances on my book tour."

The hint of a satisfied smile played around the edges of Chase's lips. "What about him?"

Bridgett warned herself not to react to Chase's smug tone and know-it-all attitude. "Martin called me several times a week."

Chase looked unimpressed as he folded his arms across his powerful chest. "Did he ever visit you?"

"Twice." Bridgett tried but failed to contain a self-conscious blush. "But he knew I was working…"

"So he was content to just wait out your return," Chase guessed.

Anticipating where this line of questioning was heading, Bridgett gritted her teeth. "Obviously."

"What about before you left?" Chase pressed, relentless as ever. "How often did the two of you see each other then?"

Bridgett shrugged. "Once or twice a week or whenever our schedules allowed."

Chase did a double take that would have been comical had it not been so irritating. "That's all?"

Bridgett regarded him steadily. "Martin and I are both very busy with our careers."

Chase inclined his head in wonderment. "That's a pretty sophisticated attitude to take."

Bridgett stiffened her spine and refused to let Chase get to her. "Martin's maturity is one of the things I like about him," she said with a smile.

Chase made no effort to contain a snort. "Is that

what it is—maturity?'' he said, nudging her ever closer to losing her composure.

Bridgett drew a calming breath. ''Just what are you implying?'' she murmured icily.

Chase looked her square in the eye. ''Every reader survey we've ever done confirms that the initial courtship phase of a relationship is the most intense. And if that's as 'intense' as it's going to get between the two of you, maybe there's a reason there has been no formal agreement of exclusivity between you. Maybe things aren't as set between the two of you as you'd like to think.''

Bridgett began to fume. So what if Martin had never said he loved her? Actions spoke louder than words. And he'd been courting her steadily and patiently for more than a year. ''You're wrong about that,'' Bridgett told Chase, the distinctly male satisfaction on his face inching her temper ever higher.

''We'll see if I am or not,'' Chase told her in a determined voice that sent a shiver of awareness shimmering down her spine. ''But I can tell you right now that until you have a bona fide marriage proposal—or in any other way link yourself exclusively to the old geezer—as far as I or any other male is concerned, the field is still wide open.''

For what? Bridgett wondered, incensed. ''You make it sound like a race,'' she said.

''Maybe it is.''

''And maybe it isn't,'' Bridgett snapped right back.

Chase merely smiled, more seductively and knowingly than ever.

Bridgett glared at him. She was not going to let him do this to her. She had gotten over whatever small crush she'd had on Chase long ago. She wasn't going to resurrect those feelings or get into a relationship with someone where her feelings might eventually be unrequited.

Harry cleared his throat loudly enough to break up the staring match between Bridgett and Chase. He looked at Winnifred. Whatever Harry and Winnifred were thinking, Bridgett noted, they were in distinct agreement.

"As long as we're talking about commitments, Bridgett," Aunt Winnifred said smoothly, breaking the uncomfortable silence, "that ring you're wearing is absolutely exquisite."

"Thank you." Bridgett breathed a sigh of relief, happy to talk about anything but Chase's sudden and unexpected pursuit of her. It wasn't like Chase to be so hot-blooded, at least not where she was concerned. She wasn't quite sure what to make of it.

"I'm guessing Martin Morganstern gave it to you?" Winnifred continued.

Bridget ignored Chase's frown. She smiled at Winnifred. "You're guessing right."

"It's not an engagement ring, though," Winnifred continued, suddenly looking just as concerned as Chase.

"More like a welcome-home present. But Martin's been hinting that a diamond engagement ring is going to follow soon," Bridgett said with some satisfaction before turning and glaring at Chase, letting him know that this was yet another goal she'd made for herself and would soon achieve. Before she knew it, her future would be secure on all counts. She had a successful career, lots of money in various investments and a gentle deferential man who adored her and wanted to build a life with her. Whether Chase Deveraux wanted to accept it or not, her life was almost set.

"What does your mother think of all this?" Winnifred asked.

Still trying to ignore the fiercely scowling Chase, Bridgett continued to speak with Winnifred. "My mom isn't exactly happy about my choice of beau."

"Because...?" Winnifred inquired as Chase got up to pace.

"My mother thinks old money and new money don't mix any better than old money and no money."

"A wise woman, your mother, and a wonderful cook, but she is dead wrong about this," Winnifred said firmly as she fingered the ruby necklace around her neck. "Money doesn't have anything to do with marrying someone. The only thing required for a happy marriage is love. So, Bridgett...do you love Martin Morganstern the way you should?"

CHASE LEANED against the mantel and waited for Bridgett's answer. It wasn't long in coming, nor was the embarrassed blush in her cheeks. "I really don't think I should be discussing my private feelings about Martin with anyone but Martin," Bridgett said stiffly.

Which meant she didn't love Martin Morganstern, after all, Chase thought. Otherwise, she wouldn't be having such a hard time saying so.

"Perhaps you're right. You shouldn't be discussing that with me," Aunt Winnie said. "But you can discuss things like the need for a formal engagement party to announce your betrothal, when the time comes. I'd love to help you and your mother with that in any way I can. In fact, we could even have your wedding and your engagement party here, if you like."

"That would be lovely, but—" Bridgett looked all the more flushed and uncertain "—Martin doesn't really want a big wedding."

"You've discussed this already?" Chase interrupted, feeling more put out than ever at the way Bridgett was about to ruin her life.

"Of course," Bridgett said before turning back to Winnifred. "And…Martin and I have decided that… given the way my mother feels about my marrying Martin, maybe the two of us should just elope."

"Nonsense. There's no way you should allow

that beau of yours to talk you out of having the wedding of your dreams,'' Winnifred said.

"I agree.'' Chase gave his opinion even though he doubted Bridgett would listen to him. ''I've been waiting a lifetime to see you all gussied up in a wedding dress, and I don't think I and everyone else who loves you should be deprived of that.''

"Somehow I knew your concern would be about you,'' Bridgett retorted dryly, giving him the kind of look that told him she thought she understood him better than anyone ever had or ever would.

The trouble was, Chase thought to himself on a troubled sigh, she didn't. She only thought she did. Because if she knew what was really in his heart and had been for a very long time now—he had just been too stubborn, too locked into the buddy relationship they'd had as kids and long since grown out of—to admit it. He hadn't wanted things to change.

Hadn't wanted to take a risk of ruining the closeness they had.

Now, realizing she was on the verge of making *the* mistake of her life, he had no such qualms. He had to do whatever was necessary to help her come to her senses. Even if it made her furious with him in the short run.

"You're wrong,'' he told Bridgett softly. ''My main concern here isn't my needs. It's you. I want you to be happy. And toward that end, I think you should take Aunt Winnie up on her offer to have both your engagement party and your wedding here in this venerable old house just as soon as possible.''

"IS SATURDAY EVENING all right with you?'' Winnifred asked Bridgett.

Bridgett blinked. She didn't know what had come over everyone. She wasn't sure she wanted to know! "This Saturday—four days from now?''

"Yes. Given the fact that you and Martin have already privately agreed the two of you should be married, I think you should make your relationship permanent as soon as possible via a formal engagement party. Just so there will be no misunderstandings of what Martin's true intentions toward you are.''

"You know, with people like me,'' Chase helped his aunt explain, "who might be wondering why the old geezer has been taking so long to claim you as his and his alone.''

Bridgett glared at him. Chase really was doing his level best to make her life difficult right now. And enjoying himself, to boot. If she didn't know better, she'd think he was jealous!

"And don't worry about your mother, dear. I'll drop by and talk to her sometime tomorrow. Between the two of us, I know we can get a party put together for you and Martin by Saturday.''

"Whoa, whoa, whoa!'' Bridgett held up a hand. "We're really getting ahead of ourselves here.''

Bridgett turned to Winnifred. "And besides, I thought you and Eleanor wanted me to be with Chase."

"We do, darling," Winnifred replied fondly. "But we also want you to realize *your* dreams. And if Martin is a part of them…"

"What's the matter, Bridgett? Think Martin might be afraid to formally commit to you?" Chase taunted.

"Actually," Bridgett replied testily, "Martin's become very impatient as of late." Uncharacteristically so, Bridgett added silently, thinking of the ultimatum her usually quite deferential beau had issued earlier in the evening during dinner.

"Well, not to worry," Chase drawled as he thrust his hands into the pockets of his shorts. "I'm sure if Marvin's the accommodating romantic you say he is, you'll have no trouble getting him to buy you a diamond and pop the question before Saturday evening."

"It's Martin, Chase, as you very well know, and the decision of when to buy a ring and pop the question should be his and his alone."

"I thought this was an equal partnership," Chase said.

"It is."

"Then if this is really what you want—" Chase looked at Bridgett determinedly "—what's holding you back? Why don't you ask him to marry you, instead of waiting for it to happen the other way around?''

Good question, Bridgett thought. It wasn't like her to be so passive. Usually she went after what she wanted with everything she had and then succeeded in getting it. But with Martin she had always been so passive. So content to let things happen at a snail's pace.

Now that she was back in Charleston near her mother and Chase and the rest of the Deveraux family, even that was starting to change.

She couldn't understand it. She had planned this so carefully. Thought about it for months now. Listed all the reasons Martin was the man for her. Why, then, was she suddenly getting cold feet now that the time was upon her to make a real commitment? Why, then, was she suddenly wondering if maybe Martin was too old for her when all along his maturity, the way he never challenged or pushed her or made her examine her motives and feelings the way Chase did, was what had appealed to her?

Aware Chase was waiting for her answer, she zeroed in on a reservation she could talk about. "Look, I'm not sure how much my mother will want to be involved in any party celebrating my betrothal to a man she doesn't think is right for me. And I don't want to put her on the spot."

"Nonsense," Winnifred said. "You're her only daughter. Of course she'll want to be involved.

She's just nervous for you, the way all mothers are nervous for their daughters.''

"With good reason in this case," Chase muttered just loud enough for Bridgett to hear as he strolled back over to the sofa where she was sitting.

Bridgett tilted up her chin and gave him a dark warning look. Chase quieted promptly, but to Bridgett's irritation did not look the least bit sorry he'd said what he had as he sat back down beside her.

Bridgett shifted slightly away from Chase. "Thank you," she told Winnifred finally. Deciding she was being silly, backtracking now, she pushed on resolutely. "To tell you the truth, Winnifred, I could use your help bringing my mother around. I really don't want to get engaged to Martin without her blessing.''

"Then I'll help you," Winnifred promised with a broad smile. She reached over and took both of Bridgett's hands in hers. "And I think the first step would be for the three of us—no make that five— let's include Grace and Amy, too, since this is an all-women soiree—should sit down tomorrow afternoon and discuss the merits of your relationship with your beau.''

"I could join in, too," Chase offered.

"Yeah, right," Bridgett said.

"I'm serious," Chase said stubbornly as Harry poured more brandy all around. "This doesn't have to be a chicks-only thing.''

"Well, it is," Bridgett said, giving Chase a look that let him know just how unwelcome his interference in this matter was.

"YOU'RE OVER HERE awfully early," Winnifred observed the next morning as Chase let himself in the back gate and joined her on the sun-drenched first-floor piazza. She put down the newspaper and looked at him over the rim of her reading glasses. "Conscience bothering you?"

"Now, Aunt Winnifred," Chase drawled, pulling up a chair at the white cast-iron-and-glass table. "Why would my conscience be bothering me?"

"Oh, I don't know. Maybe because of the way you were trying to sew seeds of doubt in Bridgett about her beau. I would have thought after the way Gabe came between you and Maggie, that would be the last thing you'd ever do to someone else."

The irony of the situation was not lost on Chase. He'd been up half the night ruminating about it and was more than a little ashamed of the nosy and intrusive way he had behaved. And yet, even knowing that, if he had the chance to do it all over again, he'd do exactly the same thing. Because watching Bridgett tie herself to Martin Morganstern was like watching an express train speed toward a break in the tracks. As much as he wanted to remain cool and detached, he couldn't stop trying to prevent Bridgett from making a mistake that would haunt her the rest of her life. Was this how Gabe had felt when he had seen Chase and Maggie? Knowing all the while that the way Maggie looked at Gabe was the way Maggie should have been looking at Chase?

"I thought you wanted to see me and Bridgett together," Chase remarked as he recalled the thinly veiled matchmaking his aunt had attempted the evening before.

"I do." Winnifred smiled at Harry as he brought Chase a cup of tea and a plate of fresh fruit and raspberry-jam-and-cream-cheese sandwiches, and just as discreetly disappeared. Winnie turned back to Chase and gave him a stern look. "I'm just not sure this is the way to go about it."

Chase knew that, too. There was a chance that if he continued on this path, Bridgett would never forgive him.

Fortunately Chase was spared further discussion of the subject by the arrival of Clyde and his Critter Removal Services truck. Chase and Harry went up to the attic of the pink-stucco mansion with Clyde to fill him in on what had gone on the night before. Clyde looked around, explaining what he was doing and why to Chase and Harry as he went, then they all headed back downstairs to give the report to Winnifred.

"You've got flying squirrels up there," Clyde told Winnifred.

"How do you know they're flying squirrels?" Winnifred asked.

"Couple reasons," Clyde said as he pocketed his flashlight and wiped his hands on the rag sticking out of his belt. "One, we've been having a lot of trouble with them this year—seems like they sneaked into just about every attic in the area over the winter. And two, they left tracks in the colony's feeding area."

"What do you mean, colony?" Winnifred asked, visibly distressed.

Clyde accepted a cup of tea, but waved off the sandwiches and fresh fruit Harry offered. "Flying squirrels nest in groups of five to seven or thereabouts. So if you've got one, you've got at least a few more."

"Oh, dear," Winnifred said.

"They've been coming in through a hole next to the chimney," Clyde continued. "I can patch that up and any other weak places, but before we do that we're going to have to set some traps."

"Do whatever you have to do." Winnifred shuddered. "Just get rid of them!"

Clyde drank the rest of his tea, then set to work. Harry disappeared, too. Chase knew he and Winnie hadn't quite finished the conversation they'd started earlier. He looked at her tenderly. Whether she liked it or not, this had to be said. "I know you mean well, Aunt Winnie, but I'm not sure we should be encouraging Bridgett to marry Martin Morganstern.'' He wasn't sure why he had goaded her into solidifying her commitment, either—except that he had hoped it would help Bridgett realize her relationship was a huge mistake.

Winnie arched one well-plucked brow. "It seems to be what Bridgett wants."

Chase shifted restlessly in his chair, irritated to find his conscience bothering him again. "Look, it's obvious she's marrying him to take the place of the father she never had."

"Their age difference really bothers you, doesn't it," Winnie murmured.

Chase scowled. "Doesn't it bother you to see her out and about with a man who is so clearly a father figure?"

"Not if she loves him."

"That's just it," Chase protested, wondering why he was the only one besides Bridgett's mother concerned about this obviously ill-fated match. "I don't think Bridgett does love that guy." Bridgett was smarter than that. The problem was, she had never gotten over not having a dad as a kid. Having someone old enough to be her father pay attention to her, well, it probably filled some void in her life. And while Chase wanted Bridgett to be happy, he didn't want her hooking up with the wrong guy for all the wrong reasons. Which was obviously what she was doing. Plus, he had a bad feeling about Morganstern. Oh, he knew the guy was an old-fashioned gentleman who said all the right things at all the right times, but on a gut level, Chase had never quite trusted him. And he didn't think Bridgett should, either. It took more than fine manners and genera-tions-old social connections to make a man.

"If you feel that way," Harry broke in as he cleared away the empty teacups. He gave Chase a man-to-man look. "You should do something about it."

Deciding Harry was right and his Aunt Winnifred wasn't, Chase headed over to his father's office at Deveraux Shipping. He caught him just before Tom headed into a meeting. "Sorry to interrupt like this," Chase told his father, "but I've got a problem and I really need to speak to you privately."

Tom ushered Chase into his office, his look openly concerned. "Your mother's okay, isn't she?"

Chase had always thought his parents still loved each other. The protective look on his father's face confirmed it. Chase shrugged. "As far as I know she is—all things considered, anyway. I'm supposed to have lunch with her and Bridgett out at the beach in a little while."

"Good." Tom relaxed visibly as he sat behind his desk. "She needs our support."

"No kidding. That job was her life."

Tom frowned in a way that reminded Chase how

much his father had always resented his mother's devotion to her broadcasting career. His lips thinning, Tom sorted through the papers on his massive mahogany desk. "What can I do for you, Chase?" he asked brusquely, knowing Chase would never have stopped by in the middle of a workday unless it was something very important.

Chase met his father's glance equably. "I need the name of a private investigator who can work quickly and quietly."

Tom stopped what he was doing. "Are you in trouble?"

"No," Chase said seriously, "but a friend of mine is."

Tom studied Chase a moment longer. Finally he said, "Talk to Jack Granger. He handles those kinds of matters for me. He'll know who you should call."

Chase thanked his dad and walked down the hall to Jack's office.

The grandson of one of their longtime employees, Jack had started working for the company when he was fourteen. He'd begun as a runner, moved to the docks and then co-op work in the executive offices. When Jack graduated from law school and passed the bar, Tom hired Jack as company counsel. It had been a good move. Jack was a quick study who already knew the shipping business and had the respect of the dock workers. And having their own lawyer had saved the company a bundle on legal fees.

There was also a bond between Tom and Jack, an understanding that seemed to go beyond work. A kinship and trust born of what, exactly, Chase didn't know. Like Tom, Jack Granger played his cards very close to his vest. Jack seemed to be the kind of guy who saw so much of what was going on behind the scenes that he knew instinctively where all the bones were buried....

And it was that kind of help, Chase thought, he was needing now.

Jack was just hanging up the phone as Chase walked in. "Your father said you needed a PI?"

Unable to help but note the Charleston newspaper spread all over Jack's desk, Chase nodded. He looked down at the photo that topped that day's gossip column. "Since when did you start reading the society page?" Chase asked curiously.

Jack flipped the page so that the Lifestyle section was closed and the photo of the beautiful blond Daisy Templeton was hidden from view. "Since I was looking for any mention of your mother being back in town," he said mildly.

Chase had the feeling Jack was hiding something. What, he didn't know. "And was there any mention?" he asked.

"Not this morning," Jack allowed with a grimace. "But with the network's announcement of your mother's firing, you can bet there will be something there tomorrow morning.''

Chase sighed, knowing how his mother felt about being the object of pity or gossip, as she had been during the divorce from his dad. ''You're probably right about that.''

Jack thumbed through his Rolodex, then scribbled down a name and number. He handed it to Chase. ''This man's expensive. But he's good.''

Again Chase had the feeling Jack was wary about revealing too much—even if Chase was Tom's son. ''You've used him before?''

Jack Granger hesitated, then said, ''Yes,'' and offered nothing more.

Telling himself it was none of his business whom his father might have wanted investigated, Chase gestured at the closed newspaper section. ''What did the article say about Daisy Templeton?''

Jack shrugged as if the subject hardly mattered to him. ''Something about Daisy taking the spring semester off…''

''Which no doubt means she got kicked out of yet another college,'' Chase said. Daisy was the bad girl of Charleston society. Not promiscuous, just wild. Always in some sort of trouble.

Jack frowned, looking suddenly protective of the wayward socialite. ''You'd think they would have better things to write about.''

''I don't know,'' Chase retorted mildly. ''Seven

pricey colleges in five years. Isn't that some kind of record?''

Jack's frown deepened. For the briefest moment he looked concerned. Which was odd, Chase thought, since Jack had no connection with the Templetons or Daisy that he knew of, anyway.

Jack tossed the paper into the trash, turned back to Chase. ''You let me know if you have any problems with the PI.''

''I will,'' Chase promised. But he didn't expect he would. If Jack Granger recommended the man, he had to be topnotch.

Chapter Seven

"Grace said you might be by and that you'd probably be peeved when you got here," Theresa observed drolly an hour and a half later when Chase strode into his parents' home. "Looks like your mother was right on both counts."

As far as he was concerned, Chase thought, he had a right to be peeved after what Bridgett had pulled. Not that he planned to discuss the matter with either his mother—or Bridgett's. No, this was between Bridgett and him.

Chase thrust his hands into the pockets of his olive-green cargo shorts. He met Theresa's eyes and forced his best what-the-hell smile. "I need to talk to Bridgett," he stated. He knew she was here. He'd seen her car parked behind the tall wrought-iron gates of his family's Meeting Street mansion when he drove up.

Theresa eyed Chase with the knowledge of a woman who had cared for him—and about him—

since birth. Finally she returned just as quietly, "She's with Grace and Paulo in the solarium."

Great, Chase thought. Not only had he been stood up by both women, he'd been stood up for another man. "Who's Paulo?" he bit out with as much indifference as he could muster.

Theresa gave Chase another long thoughtful look, then sprayed the hall table with a generous amount of furniture polish. "Paulo is the hottest yoga instructor in Charleston."

Chase's father had always been into sports—golf, tennis, waterskiing, racquetball. So had Bridgett. Not his mother. You had to twist Grace's arm to get her on the treadmill. And Grace had only done that to stay trim for TV. "Since when has my mother taken up yoga?" Chase asked.

Theresa gave her full attention to the table she was cleaning. "Since Bridgett talked her into having a lesson."

This, he had to see. He strode out of the kitchen and down the hall that ran across the back of the house. Even before he reached the solarium, he heard their fluttering voices. He rounded the corner. Walked in. And took in the twenty-something stud responsible for both women's amusement.

With his long flowing golden-brown hair, streaming well past his brawny shoulders, Paulo looked like the hero on the cover of a romance novel. He dressed like a male cover model, too—in a revealing tank top and snug-fitting gray pants.

"You may be sore tomorrow," Paulo warned Grace as he continued to knead her shoulders with an intimacy Chase found both disrespectful and totally unwarranted. "But I promise you, if you keep it up, it will all be worth it in the end."

Grace, who was still sitting cross-legged on the mat, beamed up at Paulo. "I'm sure you're right, Paulo! I feel so-o-o much better already!"

And so did Bridgett, Chase noted. *She* was practically glowing, she looked so happy and relaxed.

"Thanks for the lesson, Paulo," Bridgett said cheerfully as she mopped her face with the end of the beach towel she held in front of her. Ignoring Chase altogether, she turned and left the room.

"Are you out of your mind, hooking my mother up with that gigolo?" Chase hissed as he followed Bridgett out of the solarium and down the hall. Needing to talk to her privately, he took her by the elbow, pushed open the French doors.

Giving her no chance to protest, he steered her outside into the immaculately maintained flower garden. Sun streamed down on them, warming their bodies. The scent of flowers and saltwater—just a half a block away—teased their senses.

"No, but apparently you are out of yours." Bridgett retorted in exasperation as she pivoted to face him and dropped the towel she had been holding in front of her like a shield.

For the first time since arriving at the mansion, Chase got a good look at what Bridgett was wearing for her workout with her instructor. It was a long-sleeved pale-pink unitard that was sexy as all get-out. The clinging fabric covered her from neck to ankle, emphasizing the fullness of her breasts, the nip of her waist, the inviting curves of her hips and equally enticing slenderness of her thighs. Just looking at her made Chase's mouth go dry and his lower half pulse to life. Which was, he thought, exactly what he didn't need. An aching awareness of Bridgett as a woman, as well as a friend.

"Where do you get off, striding in there with disapproval written all over your face?" Bridgett countered indignantly as she plucked her sweat-soaked unitard away from the generous curves of her breasts. "And furthermore, you have no right to call Paulo a gigolo. He is anything but!"

Chase decided to reserve judgment on that. "Damn it, Bridgett, I don't want my mother hurt. Bad enough the network fired her after she sacrificed everything, including her marriage, for them!"

"Paulo won't hurt her," Bridgett insisted.

Chase wished he could be that sure. But if Paulo was anything like the opportunistic Romeo he appeared...

"So if that's all you wanted," Bridgett continued haughtily, starting to step past him.

"Actually it's not." Chase moved to block her way to the door. He stood with legs braced apart, arms folded in front of him, and regarded her every bit as contentiously as she regarded him. "Why did you blow off lunch with me?'' he demanded. It wasn't like Bridgett. She hadn't even called him to let him know she was canceling. He'd only found out about it when he had showed up at the restaurant they'd agreed upon and discovered—via a message from his office, no less!—that neither his mother nor Bridgett were coming after all.

Briefly guilt glittered in Bridgett's eyes, telling Chase she knew damn well how she had humiliated and angered him. ''Look, I promised you I would meet with your mother about her financial situation, and I did—over breakfast this morning,'' she said, defending herself with difficulty. ''Beyond that...'' Bridgett shrugged and her voice trailed off.

Chase passed on the opportunity to remind her that she could just as easily have called him at home or on his cell phone as she had many times over the course of their friendship. There had to be a reason she hadn't done so now, and he was pretty sure it was the same reason she had declined to share a meal with him today. He stepped closer, more aware than ever of his inability to understand women and what drove them. No matter how hard he tried, what they felt, what they wanted, were complete mysteries to him. Take last night, for instance. He'd been certain that Bridgett had wanted him to make a move on her. And that feeling had been borne out by the way she'd clung to him and kissed him back. But this afternoon she was looking at him as if she didn't know whether to slug him or forget him. So naturally he had to ask, "Did you tell Martin about the kiss?"

"No." Bridgett's teeth raked her lusciously soft lower lip. She tilted her head up to give him an even more withering glare. "And you better not, either," she warned, stepping even closer.

"Why not?" Chase taunted lightly, enjoying the way they were squaring off, toe-to-toe, as much as he always had. "Think lover boy wouldn't understand?" When Chase had been in a similar situation with Gabe and Maggie, he had been livid. Chase expected Martin to react with equal fury and jealously.

Twin spots of color appeared in her cheeks. She straightened her slender shoulders. "I think he'd be hurt if he heard something like that from you and I don't want to hurt him. Besides—" Bridgett paused and drew a deep breath as she looked him directly in the eye "—it's not as if it's going to happen again. You made your point," she concluded icily.

It was Chase's turn to be confused. He had never quite understood Bridgett and the way, as they got older, she ran so hot and cold with him. One minute acting as if he was her very best friend in the whole wide world, and the next as if she never wanted to see him again. "Which was what, exactly?" he prodded, wondering what she was getting at now.

Bridgett swallowed hard and looked both hurt and distressed. "That you'd pursue everything in a skirt, if it soothed your wounded ego, and that includes me.''

''You think that's why I kissed you—to put another notch on my belt?'' Chase stared at her in amazement, realizing Bridgett was no closer to understanding him than he was to her.

Bridgett's chin set mutinously. ''What other reason could there have been,'' she lobbed back emotionally, ''except for the fact that you saw your brother kissing your ex-fiancée yesterday and had to kiss someone just as 'inappropriate' yourself!''

What was inappropriate about him kissing her? Chase wondered, especially since she and Martin weren't officially ''exclusive.'' And, Chase was willing to bet, weren't anywhere close to being in love with each other, either. Of course, if she'd actually been engaged, she would have been off-limits and he would've had to find another way to make her see reason. But she wasn't engaged or pledged only to Martin, so he was free to use any means of persuading her he found necessary. Except maybe for the fact that they were, and had always been, friends. He drew in a long calming breath. ''My kissing you had nothing to do with Gabe's kissing Maggie,'' he explained patiently.

''Really.'' Bridget sized him up furiously. She moved forward until they stood nose to nose. ''Then why did you kiss me, Chase?''

That was just it, Chase thought uncomfortably, he didn't know. It wasn't his style to kiss a woman friend. And Bridgett was his oldest and dearest woman friend.

Aware she was waiting for an apology, he ran a hand through his hair. "You're right," he said finally. "I was out of line kissing you that way." It didn't necessarily mean he regretted it. Kissing her like that, holding her close, had made him see her in a whole new light. It had opened up possibilities that he had never really let himself consider before, but wanted very much to consider now. He had the idea Bridgett felt the same way deep down, but was too stubborn, or maybe just too afraid, to admit it. Because if they went down that road and things didn't work out just right, they could sacrifice their friendship in the process. And their friendship meant as much to him as anything in this life.

"You're darn right you were out of line last night," Bridgett agreed, and started to brush by him again.

Chase caught her arm. Determined to make amends, he said, "Look, I'm sorry if you got the wrong idea about why I did what I did."

"Are you now." Bridgett didn't look the least bit convinced that was true.

"But I want you to be happy," Chase continued sincerely.

"Then do me a favor," Bridgett said softly, wresting her arm from his grip. She looked at him with complete and utter loathing. "And don't ever—ever—kiss me again."

BRIDGETT RUSHED upstairs to change. She'd no sooner shut the guest-room door behind her, than she crossed to the bed and sank onto it, trembling. The truth was, she was just as confused about the kiss they had shared the night before as Chase obviously was. She wasn't sure why she had let him kiss her. And she sure as heck didn't know why she had kissed him back the way she had. At first it had been just shock that had kept her immobile. But then pleasure had taken over. She'd been so wowed by the soft insistence of his lips, the warmth of his hands, the sweet urgency of his tongue that she hadn't been able to resist. The truth was, she'd never felt anything like that before. Never felt passion. Never wanted so desperately for anything to continue as she had that kiss.

Oh, she had seen the fire in Chase. She had known for years what a sensual, passionate, pleasure-loving man he had grown up to be. Just as she had known he had never had, nor ever would have, any sexual or romantic interest in her. He saw her as a sister. Just as she had seen him as a brother.

Until now.

Until he had held her in his arms and showed her how wonderful the physical side of love could be.

Bridget couldn't stop thinking about the kiss.

Couldn't stop wanting another.

But that way lay folly, she knew.

Chase didn't want to marry her. Martin did. Chase didn't want to fall in love with her. He didn't want children, marriage and an enduring future with her.

Martin was ready to commit to just that—and more.

So the choice was simple.

She knew what she wanted. And she knew what Chase didn't.

"SO, WHAT IS THIS WOMAN to you, anyway?" Harlan Decker asked later that same afternoon, as soon as Chase had arrived for his appointment and explained what he wanted Harlan to do.

Chase folded his arms and regarded the burly, gray-haired man in the rumpled Hawaiian shirt and knee-length cutoffs on the other side of the desk. Harlan might come highly recommended, but he looked more like the riffraff he collared than the Charleston cop he'd once been.

"She's a friend," Chase said, knowing even as he spoke that that didn't begin to cover it. Bridgett was and always had been a big part of his life. He wasn't willing to let her go. Not when his gut told him she wasn't going to be happy marrying a blue blood who didn't know the first thing about cutting loose and having fun. Bridgett had been a mischief-loving tomboy growing up. Even though she didn't act or dress like it these days, he bet she still was, deep down. Unfortunately a society stiff like Morganstern would never appreciate that part of her.

And Bridgett, Chase thought on a wistful sigh, was a woman who deserved to be appreciated.

"I'll be blunt with you, kid." Harlan removed the digital camera he'd had slung around his neck and put it next to the straw tourist hat he'd been wearing when he walked in. He gave Chase another stern warning look. "I'm not sure this is what friends do for friends. Unless of course—" Harlan peered at Chase skeptically as he brought a cigar out of his pocket and rubbed it between his thumb and index finger "—you and this gal are more than that."

Chase shifted in his chair, wishing this meeting were already over. He hated being put on the defensive. But with time short and Harlan Decker the best there was, he didn't have much choice. "I've known her a long time, okay?" Chase said irritably. "I want to make sure she's all right."

Harlan plucked the city tour map out of his breast pocket and dropped it onto the cluttered surface of his desk. Slowly and with great care he lit the end of his cigar. He took a long drag on it and blew the smoke up in the air. "Did she ask you to do this for her?"

Fighting back an unexpected wave of guilt, Chase stared at the sunburn on Harlan's face and neck. Once again, Chase wondered if this was how Gabe had felt when he'd interfered in Chase and Maggie's walk down the aisle. Because whether Chase wanted to admit it or not, Gabe had been correct about one very important thing. Chase and Maggie never should have gotten engaged. Wanting the same things in life, wanting to be married, to start a family of your own, was simply not reason enough to hitch your future to someone else's for all eternity. Aware Harlan Decker was still waiting for an answer, Chase said tightly, "No, she didn't."

"Then you might want to reconsider before going down this path," Harlan said genially as he offered Chase a cigar.

Chase took one, wondering why Harlan was trying to make him feel remorseful. He was being gallant here, going all out to save and protect his childhood friend from making the same mistake he nearly had. "Why?" he asked as he tore the wrapper off the cigar.

"Because if the little lady finds out what you've done, she's going to resent the hell out of you," Harlan warned. "That could mean the end of your—" Harlan paused "—friendship."

Chase didn't even want to consider that. It had been tough enough as it was, losing touch with Bridgett the past few years as their careers took off and their free time dwindled to nothing. "Or, she could be grateful to me for caring enough to make sure she's all right," Chase said, envisioning how relieved Bridgett would be once she'd come to terms with the fact that his gut instinct was right and Martin Morganstern was not the man for her. Not at all.

"Beggin' your pardon, son," Harlan stated between puffs on his cigar, "but I've seen that little lady on TV promoting her book and talking investment strategy. She doesn't strike me as the type anyone, no matter how smooth, could easily bamboozle."

"Generally that's true," Chase agreed as he lit the end of his cigar. "But that was before her marriage alarm clock, or whatever the heck it is, went off and she decided it was time to settle down, pronto, even if she hadn't found the right guy yet."

"You think Morganstern wants her for her money?"

Chase shrugged and took a leisurely puff on his own cigar. "Who the heck knows? He wouldn't be the first blue blood to run his family fortune into the ground, and I've been in that art gallery of his over on King Street and seen some of the paintings he's been peddling. I can't believe he's making anywhere near what it looks like he's been spending. Bridgett, on the other hand, is rich as can be these days. And pretty and talented and sexy, to boot. So it's easy to figure out what he sees in her."

Not so easy, Chase thought, to figure out what attracted Bridgett to Morganstern. Sure, the guy was handsome enough in that impeccably dressed prettyboy way. Probably held doors open for her. Complimented her all the time, even when he didn't really mean it. And he certainly gave her lavish gifts and spared no expense when it came to entertaining

her. But did that prove he could make her happy?
The Bridgett he remembered, the Bridgett who'd
spent her youth hanging out with him and having
fun with him, would be bored to tears by a guy like
Morganstern in a year. Two, tops. And then she'd
have to divorce him, even though Bridgett had always said she didn't believe in divorce. Once two
people had decided to get married and made that
leap of faith, she believed they should stay married.

As uncomfortable as Chase was pursuing a
woman who was tied, however informally, to another guy, he couldn't just back off and let whatever
happened, happen. Bridgett's heart—heck, her
whole life!—was at stake. He had to protect her.
Had to shake some sense into her. Make her see that
Martin Morganstern was not the man for her and
would only hurt her in the end. What he couldn't
do was stand idly by and let her make a mistake of
this magnitude.

"Okay," Harlan said. "I'll check it out. What
you do with the information when I get it is up to
you."

Chapter Eight

"Winnifred is here. She and Grace are talking to your mother. And I've got to tell you, you're living dangerously, letting that tea party start without you," Tom Deveraux said when he encountered Bridgett in the east-wing hall.

"What do you mean?" Bridgett asked warily, setting her athletic bag full of sweaty workout clothes on the floor next to her feet. Amy had been invited, too—but hadn't been able to come because she had a decorating job.

"I think the three of them are about to plan an engagement party for you, with or without your permission," Tom said.

"Winnifred and Grace have talked my mother into that already?" Bridgett asked, stunned.

Tom's handsome face took on a wry grin as he allowed kindly, "Well, let's just say they're giving it their best shot. And you know how persuasive my sister and my ex-wife can be when they get their minds set on something and tackle it together."

Bridgett did indeed. Tom and Grace might have divorced thirteen years ago, but Grace remained as close to Tom's sister Winnifred as if the breakup had never occurred.

Tom paused, looking down at Bridgett with paternal concern. "Tell me the truth, Bridgett. Are you really serious about Morganstern?"

Two days ago Bridgett would have answered with a resounding yes. Now, in the wake of Chase's sudden intense interest in her and their impulsive kiss the night before, she didn't know. She kept trying to tell herself that she and the kiss did not mean anything to a playboy like Chase. She even believed it—until she recalled the tenderness of his lips and the possessiveness of his arms. And then all bets were off. She was fantasizing that there might really be something there on his part, too. Something special and wonderful and utterly romantic.

Tom led Bridgett to the seat beneath the windows at the top of the stairs so the two of them could talk privately for a moment. Together they sat down on the red velvet cushion. "Look, I know I'm not your father, but I've always tried to look out for you, anyway."

"And you've done a great job at it," Bridgett said sincerely, knowing she would never find a way to adequately express her gratitude for all Tom and Grace and indeed the entire Deveraux clan had done for her over the years. "Paying for my schooling, cheering me on at every endeavor...consoling me when I'm down.''

"Like now," Tom said gently, his love for her as evident as the wings of gray in his dark-brown hair. "I can look at your face and see something's the matter."

"I'm just confused about this whole marriage thing," Bridgett confessed as she clasped her hands tightly in her lap. "I mean, I thought I had it figured out. You pick someone who's right for you, you start dating him and then you get engaged, and before you know it you have a whole life together." It was all so simple. Or at least, Bridgett thought it should be.

"Are you engaged?" Tom nodded at the emerald ring on Bridgett's right hand.

"I could be today if I wanted to be," Bridgett said. What was it Martin had said to her the night before during dinner? *It's time for us to stop putting our careers first and concentrate on our personal lives, and have that family we have both always wanted.*

"But you're not sure you want to be engaged, is that it?" Tom studied her.

Bridgett bit her lip. She knew she could tell Tom whatever was in her heart and he would understand. "I don't want to make a mistake."

Understanding filled Tom's eyes. "There's nothing wrong with taking your time," he assured her.

"But what if that's not what I'm doing?" Bridgett asked nervously. She jumped to her feet and began to pace. "What if I'm just stalling because I'm afraid it won't work out, that he'll ditch me before we ever get to the altar, like my father ditched my mother. Or worse, we'll get married despite my reservations and then end up getting divorced."

"I guess we grown-ups haven't set a very good example for you, have we," Tom said sadly.

"You all have done fine," Bridgett said firmly, wishing she had never brought up the subject of divorce to Tom.

"I wish I thought so." For a moment Tom looked sad, like he had often since his divorce from Grace.

Again Bridgett wished she had never started this discussion. She didn't want to hurt Tom or Grace or her mom. Her real father, damn his deserting soul, was another matter. "Look, sometimes these things just happen. Sometimes things just don't work out. It doesn't have to be anyone's fault."

"You just wish you knew how to tell in advance what's going to work out and what isn't," Tom guessed sympathetically.

Bridgett nodded.

"Unfortunately there's no crystal ball we can look into that will predict the future," Tom said, comforting her. He stood and patted her on the shoulder with parental affection. "What you can rely on is your gut instinct. Or, as you ladies like to say, your intuition. It'll tell you what to do when the time comes. All you have to do is listen to it.''

TWO HOURS LATER, Bridgett was still trying to figure out how Grace and Winnifred had managed to turn her mother's attitude around so quickly when she ambled outside and saw Chase leaning against her car. He had his back to her, his cell phone pressed to his ear.

Like a bad penny—or was it a bad boy? she wondered wryly—he just kept turning up. And she had the feeling that until she either married Martin or broke up with him, it was going to keep happening.

"I saw some of the photos at the exhibit, and I have to tell you, Daisy, I really liked them." Looking as handsome and carefree as ever, with the sun glinting off his hair, Chase grinned at something Daisy apparently said. "Of course I've got an ulterior motive. Don't I always?" Chase laughed, then caught sight of Bridgett. "Listen, I've got to go. I'll call you back in a few minutes, okay?" He cut the connection and slid his cell phone back in his pocket. "That was Daisy Templeton," he said in answer to Bridgett's wordless query.

Bridgett knew of the twenty-three-year-old heiress, even though they were nearly nine years apart in age. They'd grown up in the same neighborhood of pricey historic homes along the Battery. Bridgett, a daughter of the servant class. Daisy, an unwilling member of the elite.

Bridgett moved past Chase to unlock her trunk. "A little young for you, isn't she?" she said, unable to quell the jealousy welling up in her as she tossed her athletic gear into her trunk.

Chase shrugged and made no effort to get out of Bridgett's way. "Daisy would be a tad young if I *were* interested in dating her." He held Bridgett's gaze. "I'm not."

"Either way," Bridgett returned, telling herself that was not relief she felt, not at all, "it's none of my business."

"Actually it is," Chase said genially, "since I want her to take some action photos of you and me."

Forgetting for a moment her hurry to get out of there, Bridgett asked, "Why on earth would you want her to do that?"

Chase's expression turned serious. "Because a photo op of the real you would make a great sidebar for the review I'm going to do of your new book. You know, it will show how even a buttoned-up financial counselor like you can have fun during her leisure time."

Bridgett ignored the teasing undertone in his voice, along with the hint that in her quest to become a financial and career success, she had become a stick-in-the-mud. "Why would you want to do a review of my book for women in your magazine?" she asked suspiciously.

"Because, whether you like it or not or even want

to admit it or not, Bridge, your advice is not for women only. Men can and should benefit from your considerable expertise, too.''

Privately Bridgett had been giving a lot of thought of expanding her series of financial-advice books to include a book geared specifically toward young newlyweds. A feature article in *Modern Man* magazine might reach these guys on yet another plane. Hence, at least on a purely business level, she was happy about his offer to help expand her readership in a fairly serious way. His timing and motivation, however, were suspect. She tilted her head at him, wondering if she would ever figure out what drove him. ''You're doing this to make up to me, aren't you,'' she guessed eventually.

''Maybe a little,'' Chase allowed with a sexy grin as he reached up and shut her trunk for her. ''But mostly I'm doing it because I'm a great business-person, and I know having your picture in a flash on the cover of my magazine would sell a lot of copies.''

Bridgett rolled her eyes. Leave it to a self-professed ladies' man like Chase to figure out a way to exploit the good looks she'd inherited from her mother into a business opportunity for him.

''Of course, in keeping with the theme of my magazine,'' Chase continued with a salacious wink, ''we'd want to show you're a gal who really knows how to have fun, too.''

Bridgett did her best to quash an answering grin.

"I am *not* dancing on a table with a lampshade on my head." Although she knew, under the right circumstances, Chase could probably convince her to do just that.

Chase mugged comically. "I had in mind something a little tamer."

Bridgett tried and failed to slow her suddenly thudding heart. "Such as?" she asked.

Chase's slate-blue eyes turned sentimental. "Remember when we used to go sea kayaking together when we were in college?"

Without warning, Bridgett was filled with nostalgia, too. "Over to Fort Sumter."

"Yeah." Chase gazed deeply into her eyes. He looked serious now. Hopeful. "Want to do it again?" he asked softly.

BRIDGETT WAS ABOUT to throw caution to the wind and just say yes when the back door opened and Tom Deveraux came out of the house, carrying a suitcase in one hand, a garment bag in the other. Grace followed a second later, her delicate hand upraised. "Tom!" she called after him. "Wait!"

Her face still glowing from the aftereffects of her yoga session, Grace dashed outside and caught up with Tom at the car. "I've been thinking. There's no reason for you to go back to the hotel," Grace said.

"We went over this yesterday," Tom said gravely, not caring anymore than his wife that

Chase and Bridgett could see and hear every word they were saying. "I won't have you staying in a place where you can be harassed by reporters and tourists. Besides—" Tom's expression gentled protectively, as he gazed down at his ex-wife "—you know it's easier for you to see the kids if you're here."

Looking disinclined to argue with Tom on either point, Grace said, just as courteously, "Normally when I'm here for just a few days, that's fine. But now that I'm here for good, it doesn't seem fair for me to be booting you out of your home."

"What do you suggest we do?" he asked.

"Well, why don't we both stay here?"

Beside Bridgett, Chase tensed. Bridgett knew how he felt. For all his parents' current civility in the wake of Grace's crisis, there were still times when they were just as bitter and contentious as they had been when they split, for no reason any of their children, or Bridgett or Theresa, could figure out. Hence, having them both under the same roof for an extended period of time could resurrect the bad feelings between them. Meanwhile, Tom looked just as stunned by his ex-wife's suggestion as Bridgett and Chase were.

"I don't want to feel that I'm putting you or anyone else out," Grace continued. "Realistically it's going to take at least several weeks to find a place of my own here, and probably even longer to get whatever I do eventually buy in move-in shape. So..."

"You're sure you're okay with this?" Tom said.

Grace nodded. She linked her arm through his, already steering him back toward the door, suitcases and all. "Absolutely. I want to know you're comfortable, too," she said as she led him back into the house.

Silence fell between Bridgett and Chase. Eventually Bridgett said, "Do you think there might be a chance, even a small one, that your mother's being without a job will bring your parents back together?" Bridgett had lived on the property with her mom at the time Chase's parents had split up, and she was as aware as Chase that his parents hadn't always been able to be cordial to each other since the divorce. Eventually things had calmed down between Tom and Grace, of course, but for a while there had been a lot of tension. No one, though, had ever found out what, exactly, caused their divorce, since neither Grace nor Tom would say. All anyone knew, including their own children, was that they had differences that simply couldn't be resolved. Period.

"I wouldn't even want to speculate about that," Chase said, his expression turning grim again. He turned back to Bridgett, forced a smile. "And speaking of unknowns, you never did tell me how that tea party went."

Now it was Bridgett's turn to grimace. "Your

aunt and both our mothers have joined forces to throw a party here on Saturday evening. Martin and I are the guests of honor.''

''Well,'' Chase said after a moment, looking just as unhappy as she felt, ''that's what you wanted.''

Was it? *Be careful what you wish for—you just might get it.* ''Maybe,'' Bridgett allowed, doing her best to keep her conflicted emotions in check, ''if I didn't feel like I were such a victim of reverse psychology, at least on my mother's part.''

''You think she's not sincere about wishing you and Martin well in your...whatever it is,'' Chase said.

Bridgett shrugged, knowing if anyone could understand this, it was Chase. ''I think deep down my mother doesn't feel, because of our different backgrounds, that Martin will ever marry me. But Winnie and your mom have talked her into at least giving Martin a chance to prove his devotion to me and just see what happens. Your mother, in particular, thinks a happy marriage is worth the risk. She convinced my mother to just step back and let me follow my heart, knowing that whatever I eventually decide, my mom will be in my corner, backing me up and cheering me on.''

Chase swallowed. Emotion crept into his voice, tenderness into his eyes. ''My mom said that?''

''Yeah.'' Bridgett sighed, feeling quite nonplussed. She turned her face up to Chase. ''Strange, isn't it, to have her so clearly pro marriage, especially as she divorced your dad over his initially pretty vehement protestations.''

Chase nodded in a way that reminded Bridgett how hard he, too, had fought against his parents' divorce, both at the time and later, in the years immediately following the breakup. To no avail. Once the divorce decree was issued, Tom and Grace never made any move to reconcile or explain why they had done what they had. "What about Aunt Winnifred?" Chase asked. "What persuasive argument did she give to change your mother's mind?"

"Exactly what you'd expect from anyone who was widowed after just a year of marriage to the love of her life. She thinks time—for any two people in love—is simply too short. And that I should savor whatever it is I've found with Martin or anyone else, because before I know it, it could all be taken away from me."

Chase sighed. "Poor Aunt Winnie. She's never gotten over losing her husband."

"I know," Bridgett murmured.

A companionable silence fell between them, reminding Bridgett of all she and Chase had once shared. There'd been a time when they could talk about anything. Was it possible they could get that closeness back? And if they did, how would that affect her relationship with Martin? Although he'd never been the jealous type, she wasn't sure Martin would appreciate or approve of any renewed intimacy between Bridgett and Chase.

"So what does Martin think of all this?" Chase asked, abruptly looking as pensive and sentimental as she felt.

"I don't know." Bridgett felt herself tense again and she turned away from Chase's probing gaze. She felt suddenly disloyal to Martin for having talked to Chase about the party first. "I haven't told him yet."

"WHY LEAVE IT at just a gala in our honor?" Martin said, when Bridgett told him. "Why not make it something really special by announcing our wedding date that night?"

Bridgett sucked in a breath. No doubt about it. Her world, which for years had chugged along at a snail's pace, was suddenly moving way too fast. "Because we're not engaged yet," she said calmly, wondering when these precommitment jitters would go away. Were she and Martin meant to marry? Or would they be better off as friends? Bridgett was too nervous to know. Martin, however, had no such qualms.

"All you have to do is let me buy you a diamond, and we will be." Martin took Bridgett into his arms. Before he could kiss her or even attempt to, Bridgett found herself turning her head. Another first for her. Martin's expressions of affection hadn't been all that frequent, but she'd never rebuffed them—until now.

Then again, she'd never kissed anyone else since

she and Martin had started dating each other—except for Chase. Guilt flooded Bridgett as she extricated herself from Martin's tender embrace. She had been putting off telling him about the kiss, but she knew she couldn't do it any longer. As the man who wanted to marry her, he deserved to be told the truth about her mistake. She put several feet of space between them, folded her arms tightly in front of her and struggled for the courage she needed. "There are things you don't know about me, Martin," she told him softly.

Martin smiled and sat on the edge of his desk in the Morganstern Gallery office, looking as relaxed and genial as ever. "I know everything I need to know. You're smart and pretty and kind and loving, successful in your own right. You're everything I ever wanted in a woman, everything I thought I'd never find. I know people have been filling your head with doubt because I waited so long to marry. But there's no reason for you to be upset about that," he told her firmly and straightforwardly. "The thirteen-year difference in our ages is not going to be a problem. I promise you, I'll see to it you always have what you need, in every respect."

Bridgett looked at Martin, trying to find strength in his cool self-assured presence. "I know you will." She smiled back at him, still struggling with her conscience. Martin had been so good to her. The last thing she ever wanted to do was hurt or betray him.

Martin took her hand and led her to the sofa, where they both sat down. "Then meet me at King Street Jeweler's tomorrow morning. And help me pick out a ring."

Once again Chase disrupted her ability to make plans with Martin.

"I can't," Bridgett admitted reluctantly. "I promised Chase Deveraux I'd do this sea-kayaking photo shoot for his magazine." Briefly Bridgett explained Chase's plans to review and further publicize her latest bestseller.

Instead of being jealous or the least bit put out, Martin smiled. "That sounds like a great publicity opportunity for you," he said, his approval evident. "It should really help sales of your new book."

Shouldn't her soon-to-be fiancé be jealous that she was ditching him for Chase? Bridgett wondered silently. Especially when Martin was trying at long last to formalize their relationship by buying her a ring? Shouldn't he at least sense something amiss, especially when Bridgett was so sick with guilt over the forbidden kiss that she could barely stand it? Then again, maybe she was the one making too much of things. As Chase had pointed out to her, she and Martin had no formal commitment to each other just yet. No promise of exclusivity had been made, even though Bridgett had more or less been adhering to that ever since Martin and she had started dating. She assumed Martin had done the same, but the truth was, she didn't really know what he'd done during the three months she had been off promoting her book. And she hadn't been curious enough to ask.

As for her unexpected interlude with Chase the night before…well, she was smart enough to know that kiss, sensual as it had been, had meant no more to Chase than any other pass he'd made at any other woman. And she had made it very clear to Chase that he wasn't to put the moves on her again. So the likelihood was, nothing else of a romantic nature would happen tomorrow when they went sea kayaking together, particularly since they were going to have Charleston Wild Child Daisy Templeton as their twenty-three-year-old chaperone.

And if it didn't happen again, what would be the point of telling Martin, especially as it was bound to hurt him?

"Do you think you'll be free late tomorrow afternoon, say, around four-thirty?" Martin continued, oblivious to her conflicted thoughts.

Keep your eye on the future. On the man who wants you and will marry you. Bridgett looked at Martin and forced a smile. She couldn't let Chase lure her into a mistake, the way he had once seduced her into mischief, just because wicked fun or rollicking good times lay ahead. She was too old for that. Too focused on what she needed and wanted, which was marriage, stability, family and a future happiness that would last. Martin was offering her all those things. Chase wasn't.

"I'm sure we'll be finished long before then," she said.

"Then we'll meet at the jeweler's tomorrow," Martin said firmly. "And make this relationship of ours official."

Chapter Nine

Bridgett couldn't believe it. Chase wasn't even dressed. In fact, Bridgett noted with growing pique, he looked as if he had just that moment stumbled out of bed. Which was odd, because Chase could usually be counted on to be prompt. Bridgett's brows drew together. "Did I get the time wrong?" she asked.

"Nope." Chase consulted the clock on the wall behind him. "You were supposed to be here at seven-thirty and it's…seven twenty-nine."

"Then how come," Bridgett questioned as he ushered her inside his beachhouse, "you're still wearing your pajamas?" Actually, it was just a pair of incredibly sexy pajama bottoms, with a drawstring waist that rode just below his navel and seductively showcased his lean hips and long legs.

"Daisy's idea." Chase yawned as he lifted his arms and lazily raked his fingers through the mussed waves of his dark-brown hair. Apparently he had no compunction at all about shifting the blame. "She wanted me to look as if I was just waking up when she took the photos of me that are going to appear on the introductory page, along with my monthly letter to the readers.''

Bridgett glared at him. She had gotten up at the crack of dawn after a late night out with Martin socializing, rushed to shower and do her hair, endured a wardrobe crisis that sent her into a tizzy, and then driven all the way out to the beach at top speed, only to find Chase still in bed! And from the looks of his rumpled hair, drowsy eyes, unshaven jaw and the time he had taken to greet her, he had still been sleeping soundly when she rang the bell. ''You should have told me you weren't going to be ready at seven-thirty,'' Bridgett said. ''Then I could have arrived later.''

''We needed you here.'' Daisy Templeton bounded up on the deck of Chase's beachhouse and over to where Chase and Bridgett were standing. ''We're going to photograph you waking Chase up, tugging off the covers and pulling him out of bed. Sort of fits with the theme of his magazine, don't you think?''

''The theme of impossibly irritating men?'' Bridgett said.

Daisy grinned. At twenty-three the dazzling blonde was evidently young enough not to mind Chase's playboy image. Or the way he constantly pushed women's buttons.

''Come on.'' Daisy took Chase by the hand and

led him through a living space that included a den
with a fireplace and sofa, kitchen and dining area
all in one, to the loft upstairs. "Let's get you back
under those covers before you wake up anymore.
Bridgett, you come, too."

Bridgett sighed, set down her shoulder bag and
car keys, and marched up the stairs after them. By
the time she got up there, Chase was lying facedown
on the bed, the covers draped artfully over his legs.
His arms were folded beneath his pillow. He had
his head turned slightly to the side. His back and
shoulders were beautifully bare, all sculpted muscle
and smooth suntanned skin. Just seeing him that
way made Bridgett's mouth go dry.

"What do you think, Chase?" Daisy said, as she
snapped pictures. "Should we have her stretch out
beside you?"

Bridgett's insides fluttered at the thought of being
on the bed with him. The last thing she wanted to
do was roll around under the covers with Chase.
Nearly engaged or not, it might give him ideas.
Heck, it might give *her* ideas!

Chase grinned, opened one eye and trained it on
Bridgett. "Ol' Marvin might object to that," he
drawled.

"It's Martin." Bridgett pushed the words through
clenched teeth. "And he would have every right to
object." She grabbed the sheet beneath Chase's
middle and tugged it free. Knowing even as she did
so that it was less about her following the directions

of Chase and his college-kid photographer than getting Chase up and out of that bed of his.

Daisy stopped snapping long enough to turn her incredulous gaze to Bridgett. "You're not dating Martin Morganstern, are you?"

"Yes," Bridgett said, as her temper burned ever hotter. "Why?"

"Because he's—" Daisy hedged uncomfortably, her camera still cradled in her hands "—I was going to say…ancient."

The heat of her embarrassment crept into Bridgett's cheeks. Ignoring Chase's I-told-you-so smirk, Bridgett turned back to Daisy. "Martin is not that old," she said stiffly before the notoriously reckless Daisy could blurt out anything even more insulting.

"I think he is," Chase said, rolling onto his side. The covers slid down even more as he stretched his long legs. He eyed Bridgett in a goading manner. "I think he's way too old for you. And a stick-in-the-mud, as well."

Bridgett propped her hands on her hips. Compared to Chase, Martin did seem old. But then, wasn't that the point—for her to marry someone dependable and mature? Someone she could count on not to run out on her the way a sexy young guy like Chase might?

"Are we going sea kayaking or not?" she demanded as Daisy went back to snapping away what would likely turn out to be a highly amusing photo essay.

"Sure," Chase said. He checked Bridgett out in a leisurely male fashion that made her pulse pound. His smile widened even more. "Right away."

"How LONG IS THIS going to take?" Bridgett asked as they fastened their bright-yellow safety vests, pushed their kayaks out into the channel between Sullivan's Island and Fort Sumter and climbed in.

"The usual, I suspect," Chase said as Daisy continued to take action photos of them from the beach. "About half an hour to kayak over to Fort Sumter, a while to mess around once we're there and half an hour or so back here."

"Fine," Bridgett said, aware it was already after nine and all they'd managed to do was get her so riled up she wanted to scream. She set her jaw and tried to have a good time as she settled comfortably in the seat of her kayak. "Just as long as we're done by three-thirty." In the distance, Daisy climbed into the speedboat that would follow the two of them from a distance and allow her to take photos of them as they crossed to the man-made island in Charleston Harbor upon which Fort Sumter had been built.

Chase paused long enough to give Daisy and her hired-boat pilot a salutary wave, then turned back to Bridgett. "What happens at three-thirty?" he asked curiously.

Bridgett dipped one end of her oar in the water, then the other, beginning the practiced rhythm that soon had her gliding through the water with ease.

"I need to go home and get a shower," she told Chase as the spring sun beat down on them. "I'm meeting Martin downtown at four-thirty."

"Getting the Senior Citizen Special for dinner, huh?"

Bridgett accidentally-on-purpose used her oar to splash water on him. "Very funny," she said. "And no, we are not planning to eat dinner that early."

The muscles in his brawny shoulders rippling smoothly, Chase paddled hard enough to take the lead. "Going to help him pick out a pair of orthopedic dress shoes?" he said as he sent an arc of water across her face and chest.

Bridgett paddled harder and faster. She kept her eyes straight ahead as she drew even with Chase again. "Wrong again, bucko," she told him with a great deal more satisfaction than was warranted. "We're going to pick out my engagement ring."

Chase stopped paddling and slanted her an astounded look. "He asked you to marry him last night?"

"Not exactly." Bridgett slowed down, too, as she blinked the water from her eyes.

"If he didn't propose—" Chase narrowed his glance at her as he paced his paddling to stay exactly even with her "—then why are you picking out a ring?"

Bridgett concentrated on the soothing rhythm of their oars hitting the water.

"Because it's time," Bridgett said stubbornly, refusing to let Chase goad her into feeling let down by the matter-of-fact way events were unfolding.

"Well, that's an amazingly pragmatic attitude to have," Chase said grimly as they drew ever nearer to the small beach.

"What do you mean by that?" Bridgett discovered she was gritting her teeth again as she watched a tour boat, crowded with people, pull up next to the burned-out ruins of Fort Sumter.

Chase shrugged. "I just figured you'd have wanted some highly romantic proposal, you know, some great big deal when Marvin actually asked you to marry him. I expected him to surprise you with a ring, not just set an appointment and take you to pick out one."

Bridgett knew she didn't have to defend herself to Chase and probably shouldn't even try. But before she realized it, the know-it-all look on Chase's face had her opening her mouth again. "Look, there was no reason for Martin to get down on bended knee when we both know what we want."

"I'd think, if he wants to marry you so much, that's exactly what he'd do," Chase said, looking disappointed for her.

"Is that what you did for Maggie?" she challenged as she paddled right up onto the beach.

"No." Chase sighed. "Although," he allowed as he dragged his kayak up onto the sand out of harm's way, "maybe if I'd made more of a fool of myself over her, she wouldn't have dumped me for my brother.''

"And maybe," Bridgett said as she braced both her hands on the lip of her kayak and levered her way out, "your marriage to her just wasn't meant to be, after all.''

Chase reached over and helped Bridgett pull her kayak out of the water and up onto the narrow beach beside his. Silence fell between them as he looked at her appraisingly. Then he grinned at her in the way he always did when trouble was coming. "And maybe neither you nor I are really the marrying kind," he asserted just as strongly.

Bridgett flushed self-consciously. "What's that supposed to mean?" she demanded as she reached for the water bottle in her pack.

"Well, think about it." Chase pulled a bottle of a popular sports drink from his pack, too. "Except for my mistake with Maggie and yours with Morganstern—"

"My relationship with Martin is not a mistake," Bridgett snapped. Her temper had begun to flare.

"—neither of us has ever been close to tying the knot." Chase inclined his head at her. As his gaze drifted over her face, his eyes warmed even more. "Don't you think that should tell us something?"

Bridgett planted her bare feet even more firmly in the sand. "Like we're cautious?"

"Ah, but we're not cautious, Bridgett, either of us." Chase kept his eyes on the flushed contours of her face. "'Cause if we were, we would have selected safe and easy career paths. Instead, we both struck out on our own, risked everything we had and built two very successful businesses out of nothing but our own desire in a few years' time."

Bridgett dropped her water bottle back into her bag and plucked out a pair of sneakers. She brushed the sand off her feet and slipped them on. "Just because I take some pretty big risks in my professional life doesn't mean I take them in my personal life," she said pointedly. "Now come on. Let's have some fun."

CHASE WASN'T SURE why he'd started this, other than to distract Bridgett and keep her from doing anything rash like accepting a marriage proposal from Martin. He knew that everything he was saying was pure bull. But when she looked at him like that and went toe-to-toe with him, challenging everything he said and did, Chase couldn't help but get into the banter. He'd missed matching wits with Bridgett. Missed her—more than he'd known. The question was, how was he going to keep her from slipping out of his life as easily as she had slipped back in?

"What?" Bridgett said once she'd finished tying her shoes and straightened up to square off with him again. "No smart remark?"

Chase tore his eyes from the bare silky skin of her slender shoulders and the sexy indentation of her collarbone. "I'm thinking." He lifted the plastic bottle to his lips and drank deeply of the chilled liquid.

"About...?" Bridgett prodded.

"The two of us," Chase slipped back into the banter that was as comforting as it was familiar. "And why we're just not suited for marriage," Chase said in response, liking the angry sparkle in her eyes. There was nothing more alluring, in his opinion, than Bridgett, out to prove a point.

"Back to that again," Bridgett said, giving him her full attention.

Chase brought out a pair of nicely broken-in deck shoes and slipped them on. "We're cut out for fun, Bridgett."

"So?" Bridgett rolled her eyes in exasperation as he recapped his bottle and tossed it back into his pack.

Enjoying the feel of the spring breeze on his body, Chase braced his hands on his waist. He looked at Bridgett seriously. "So, marriage is all rules and responsibility, obligations and expectations."

Bridgett raked her lower lip with the edge of her teeth. "And the single life is...?"

Chase picked up the oars and set them in the wells of their kayaks. "Full of excitement and adventure."

"And a lot of lonely nights," Bridgett added,

frowning as she rubbed her index finger across her lips.

"Doesn't have to be that way," Chase disagreed. "Not anymore. You can always call me."

"And then what?" Bridgett rummaged in her pack and finally plucked out a tube of lip balm.

Chase swallowed as he watched her slowly stroke it on her lips, then offer it to him. "Oh, I'm sure we could find some mischief to get into," he added dryly as he put the tube to his mouth and ran it over his lips much more swiftly than she had done.

"I'm sure we could," Bridgett agreed sagely. "I'm just not sure we should."

"You've got to cut loose again and set yourself free," Chase advised her cavalierly, aware his lips now tasted like a combination of wintergreen-flavored balm and Bridgett. He pressed the tube back into the palm of her hand and frowned as the heat of her skin sent an even more potent charge barreling through him.

Bridgett narrowed her eyes at him, then continued in a soft low tone, "Tell me something. Does this speech work on most women, Chase? 'Cause it's not working on me."

Chase laid a hand over his heart and regarded her with mock pain. "I'm hurt," he said with only a twinge of guilt. Because the truth of the matter was, he was beginning to think he'd do literally anything to get her away from tying herself to Martin.

"I want to settle down with a nice guy and never

have to worry about a dateless Saturday night again.''

Chase shrugged. ''I'm a nice guy.''

''With a very short attention span when it comes to the fairer sex.'' Bridgett dug the toe of her sneaker into the sand and turned her attention back to the water lapping at the shore. She brushed the hair from her eyes and frowned back at him. ''How many women have you dated, anyway?''

''I don't know.'' Chase shrugged uncaringly. ''Fifty.''

Bridgett's brow arched in cool disbelief.

''A hundred,'' Chase amended.

Her brow climbed even higher. ''Try a couple of hundred,'' she corrected dryly.

Chase refused to feel guilty about that. Sure, he'd had a lot of evenings with a lot of other women, but his dates with those women were as forgettable as they had been superficial. Women wanted to be with him because he was successful. Whereas he had been looking to fill lonely hours. He smiled at Bridgett and continued truthfully, ''Which just goes to show that I'll take out just about anyone who's in need of a little diversion.''

''Providing, of course, she's beautiful and sexy, to boot.''

Chase opened his mouth to disagree, then shut it again. He'd never really thought about it and certainly a woman's looks weren't the basis for any friendship he'd ever had, but he supposed Bridgett had a point. "Actually," he allowed with a disarming shrug, "it's really a woman's personality I'm interested in."

Bridgett threw back her head and laughed.

"It just doesn't matter if she looks great, too," Chase continued easily, figuring there was no reason to fudge about it. He did prefer the company of a beautiful woman. And in his estimation, there was no woman on earth more beautiful than Bridgett Owens. He leaned closer and looked down his nose at her. "Not that I've seen you dating anyone who was missing the handsome gene, either."

"Oh, really, and what kind of men do I date, since you're such an expert on me?" Bridgett scoffed.

"The handsome, successful, exceedingly reliable and responsible type. The type who wouldn't know how to have fun if it stared 'em in the face." The type, Chase thought, who set his teeth on edge, they were so completely wrong for her.

Bridgett smiled at him slyly. "I think you'd be surprised at some of the fun I've had."

Jealousy struck like a craw in his gut. The thought of Bridgett having the time of her life with someone else was curiously almost more than he could bear. Suddenly struggling with completely unwarranted feelings of protectiveness, coupled with the urge to take Bridgett in his arms, say to heck with everything he was trying to accomplish here—namely, bringing her to her senses—and just kiss her madly,

Chase turned back to the water to scarch out Daisy and the blessed distraction and chaperoning presence she offered.

She was still some distance away, perched comfortably in the boat she'd hired, snapping photos. In desperate need of immediate diversion, Chase waved her in.

"YOU'RE AWFULLY SOLEMN," Bridgett observed short minutes later as they joined the other tourists streaming toward the park ranger standing in the grassy center of the former parade grounds, located inside what was left of the five-foot-thick walls of the old brick fort.

Probably because I just realized my feelings for you aren't as simple and uncomplicated as I thought they were, Chase thought as he tipped his head down at her. *And I'm not sure if you're ready to deal with that any more than I am.* "It's a solemn place," he said with a shrug as they surveyed the ruins of the former military installation. Daisy followed a discreet distance behind them, taking photos.

Mindful of the unevenness of the terrain beneath their feet, Chase reached over and took Bridgett's arm. He swallowed hard against the building knot of sentiment in his throat, more aware than ever of all that was at stake. "The first battle of the Civil War was fought here, you know."

"Somehow I think it's more than that," Bridgett

persisted with a flicker of concern in her deep-brown eyes.

Bridgett always had been able to read him, more than anyone else, Chase thought. He took her by the hand and led her away from the park ranger, who was telling how the fort had been built to protect the harbor. "I was just thinking how much I've missed hanging out with you," he said honestly as they checked out the three cannons and the mortar on the parade ground, as well as the projectiles imbedded in the wall in front of the guns. When they were teenagers, they had kayaked over here frequently, spent countless hours on the beach. They knew all the history, as well as every nook and cranny of the old fort.

"We did have a lot of fun when we were growing up," Bridgett admitted with a wistfulness that warmed his soul as they toured the ruins of the officers' quarters.

Chase turned to face her. She had never looked more beautiful than she did at that moment, standing there in a clinging hot-pink swimsuit and black nylon shorts. Her cheeks were ripe with color, her lips soft and bare. The seabreeze ruffled her auburn hair, pulling tendrils from the neat French braid onto her face and the nape of her neck.

He moved a strand of hair from her face and tucked it behind her ear. His mood suddenly as pensive and wistful as hers, he asked, "How did we lose touch with each other?"

Bridgett shrugged and headed up the stairs to the observation deck that overlooked the bay. The set of her lips turned as melancholy as her voice. "Our lives went in different directions."

"It's more than that."

"Is it?" Bridgett turned so her back was to the metal railing. Like him, she seemed to be struggling with her feelings, both about what their relationship had been and what it might or might not become. "You were starting a magazine from scratch. And you had a very active social life, to say the least."

Chase grinned at the note of jealousy in her voice. He'd known her a lot of years. He'd never seen her look at him quite that way.

"The point is," Bridgett continued, "you were so darned busy it didn't leave much time for the two of us to pal around."

Chase supposed that was true. In the aftermath of his called-off wedding, he had been avoiding anyone who was close to him and might want to "talk." No one had been closer to him, no one had known his moods better, than Bridgett. Not about to take all the blame, however, he pointed out softly, "You're at fault for the lapse in our friendship, too."

Bridgett's expression grew even more introspective. "You're right. I have let my career take up all my time and energy, too." She was silent as she looked out over the water, first toward the beach on Sullivan's Island, where his house was located, and then toward the many beautiful mansions along the Battery, where his Aunt Winnifred lived. "We have to face it, Chase, even if we don't want to." Bridgett pivoted slightly away from him and studied the place where the Ashley and Cooper rivers came together. "You and I have both changed."

"Maybe not as much as you think." Chase put his hands on her shoulders and turned her so that she had to face him. When their eyes met, he continued pragmatically, telling her what he was pretty sure she already knew. "That guy in my magazine—the ultimate bachelor all the papers write about—isn't the real me."

Bridgett searched his face. "Then why do you portray yourself that way?"

Chase shrugged and reluctantly let his hands fall back to his sides. "For exactly the reason you portray yourself as the ultimate female investor. Because dedicated perfection, in any venue, appeals to the buying public."

Bridgett's lips came together in a delicate scowl. "But my advice to people helps them, Chase."

Not about to let her get away with that false assumption, Chase grinned and chided, "I printed a knockout recipe for grilled hot wings just last month. As well as a guide for getting girlfriends to enjoy sports as much as guys do. Now if those two things together won't bring about world peace, I don't know what will."

Bridgett rolled her eyes. "You always did have a way of twisting things around to your advantage."

"And you always had a way of worrying way too much," Chase said, thinking he had never wanted to haul a woman into his arms and kiss her senseless as much as he wanted to kiss Bridgett at that very moment.

Bridgett's eyes widened. Her lips parted. She swayed toward him, chin tilted up to his. Chase brought his hands to her shoulders. And damn it all if he wouldn't have said to heck with her cautions not to ever kiss her again had they not suddenly been invaded by a noisy group of fourth-graders.

Bridgett jerked away, blushing furiously.

Chase dropped his hands and stepped back even as he silently and vehemently condemned the interruption.

Before they had a chance to catch their breaths, Daisy joined them once again. "Stay right where you are!" she shouted above the cacophony of two hundred schoolchildren on a field trip. "I love these action shots!"

Chase would have settled for a little less action. He would have settled for having Bridgett in his arms again. Her mouth against his—soft, warm and pliant. But wasn't that just the way…

"YOUR NOSE IS sunburned," Martin said when Bridgett joined him at King Street Jeweler's later that afternoon.

So were numerous other parts of her body, Bridgett thought, already beginning to feel the sting. She had no doubt she would be in agony by the end of the evening. But not wanting to ruin what should be a very exciting moment of her betrothal, she said in explanation, "I think my sunblock wore off in a couple places." Like her chest, back and legs. "The sea-kayaking photo shoot took a little longer than I thought it would."

"How'd that go, anyway?" Martin held out a straight-backed velvet chair.

Bridgett slid into it gracefully, tucking her skirt around her legs. "It was great, except for the two hundred fourth-graders that overran the place at the end." She smiled, remembering the pandemonium. "Chase and Daisy and I about got trampled in the stampede."

"I can't wait until we have a fourth-grader of our own," Martin said.

A week ago Bridgett would have been delighted at the thought of having children with Martin. Now…all she could think about was what they'd have to do together to make a baby. Deciding there was no reason for her to be worrying about *that* now, Bridgett hastily changed the subject, as well as the direction of her thoughts. "Did you find any rings you liked?"

"Yes, as a matter of fact." Martin pointed out a pear-shaped four-carat ring. "What do you think?"

Bridgett studied it with a critical eye, knowing

that Chase would never in a million years pick out something that ostentatious. Finally she said honestly, "Too cumbersome."

Martin scaled it down to a three-carat marquis.

Bridgett wondered how Martin could be so out of touch with her taste after a year of courting. Again she shook her head, admitting quietly, "I just don't like the shape."

They tried a square, an oval. Large. Small. Platinum and gold. Nothing appealed to Bridgett, even though they were all exquisitely beautiful rings. Eventually Martin turned to her in frustration.

"You're not going to like anything today, are you," he guessed.

"They just don't seem right." *We just don't seem right,* Bridgett thought uneasily and then immediately wondered what was happening to her. Until Chase had come back into her life, she'd been certain she and Martin would marry. They'd both have fulfilling careers and settle right here in Charleston. They'd have two children, a girl and a boy, a beautiful home in the city and another smaller, cozier place at the beach. Their life together was going to be serene and perfect and scandal-free. Her children would be neither illegitimate nor the victims of a divorce. Her children would be safe and protected from all that pain and embarrassment. So why, suddenly, was her vision of the future so murky? Why was she filled with doubts?

Martin studied her. "You want to be surprised,

don't you," he said thoughtfully after a moment. "In fact, you should be surprised. Buying you a ring this way is too…unromantic."

Which was, Bridgett thought uneasily, exactly what Chase had said.

Chapter Ten

"You kissed Chase," Amy Deveraux repeated incredulously at seven that evening when she'd come by to finish up a spring redecorating project Bridgett had commissioned before she left for her book tour.

"Chase kissed me," Bridgett corrected as she and Amy searched for a place to hang the brilliantly colored seascape Amy had found. "Then I kissed him back."

"And...?" Amy looked as if she could barely believe what she was hearing.

"And nothing," Bridgett said, trying not to feel disappointed as she took down the framed poster that had been hanging above her piano and replaced it with the painting. "We both said it was a mistake."

"Chase said that?" Amy regarded Bridgett skeptically.

"Well, I said it," Bridgett admitted as she put her poster aside for use in another room, "and he had no choice but to agree, because I'm going to marry Martin.''

"Right." Amy rolled out a rug of sage-green, pale yellow and cream in the center of Bridgett's second-floor living room.

Bridgett sighed in exasperation as she helped return the coffee table and two wing chairs to their positions. "Not you, too!"

Amy shot her a sisterly glance as she moved a large vase of sea oats closer to the black-marble fireplace. "Martin is awfully old for you, Bridgett."

"Thirteen years is not that much older," Bridgett said stiffly. And Bridgett was getting tired of making the argument.

Amy lifted a dissenting brow, at that moment looking very much like she sided with her brother Chase. "Maybe not for some couples, if one person is slow to mature and the other is exceptionally fast," Amy allowed cautiously, "but Martin seems like he's from a completely different generation!"

Which was, Bridgett thought, sighing inwardly, like saying he was old enough to be her father. Something else she had heard again and again. Bridgett brushed the hair off her forehead, then deciding she needed to get it off her face altogether, she slipped into her bedroom and pulled her hair up into a ponytail. "Our life experiences have been different. But our fundamental values are the same."

"Don't get me wrong. I'm not knocking good values. I think every prospective beau should have them.'' Amy paused in the doorway to Bridgett's bedroom, her shoulder against the frame. ''But don't you want a lot more in a beau than shared values?''

Bridgett blotted the perspiration from her brow with the back of her hand and walked back out into the living room to join Amy. ''I can count on Martin, Amy. I love your brother—I love all you guys.'' The Deverauxs were as much her family as her mother. ''But I don't think I could ever count on Chase,'' Bridgett continued, wishing the opposite were true. ''Not the way I'd need to, anyway.'' He might hang out with her for a while if she stopped seeing Martin, but the next time a pretty girl came along, off he'd go. And then she'd be alone again, pining after someone who was destined to be her friend and nothing more.

Amy looked unhappy, but much to Bridgett's disappointment, she didn't disagree with Bridgett's harsh assessment of Chase and his notoriously short attention span when it came women. ''What does Martin say about all this? Have you told him what happened between you and Chase?'' Amy asked gently, bringing out a vase of dried flowers and sea grasses and placing it on the piano.

A warm flush climbed from Bridgett's throat to her face as she helped Amy take off the wintry red-velvet slipcovers on Bridgett's furniture and replace them with slipcovers in a springlike fabric. Guilt warred with her need to keep her life running smoothly and without conflict. ''I tried,'' she admitted, exasperated, "but he kept interrupting. Finally—" Bridgett let out a shaky breath and crossed her arms "—it just…it didn't seem like the right time. But I know I have to come clean with him." And she knew, for all their sakes, that she had to do it soon.

Amy slanted her a worried glance. Her turquoise-blue eyes probed Bridgett's face relentlessly. "Sure about that?"

"Amy, I can't accept an engagement ring from him with a secret like that between us. It would be dishonest." Which was, Bridgett admitted to herself unhappily as she rolled up her old slipcovers and put them aside for cleaning, the real reason she hadn't been able to pick out a ring that afternoon at the jeweler's. Martin thought she was just being picky, that she'd been disappointed because he hadn't been more romantic, but she knew it was more than that. Much more. Her reservations about making a commitment to Martin—any kind of a commitment—were beginning to feel overwhelming. She wanted to think it was just an early case of prewedding jitters, but she had a sneaking suspicion it was more than that. And if that was the case, then it meant everyone else was right and she was wrong.

Amy shrugged as if Bridgett's kiss with Amy's brother Chase was not the big deal Bridgett kept telling herself it had been. "Well, I don't see why you have to tell Martin about a kiss that didn't mean anything, anyway,'' Amy said, continuing to regard Bridgett sternly. "You said it's never going to happen again." Amy ripped off the tags and added coordinating throw pillows to Bridgett's newly covered sofa.

"It won't happen again," Bridgett said bluntly. "Chase understands that." He knew as well as she did that if they ventured down that road, it could destroy their friendship. She was certain Chase didn't want that any more than she did, especially now that they were beginning to get close again.

Amy stopped what she was doing and propped her hands on her hips. "Then what would telling Martin accomplish, besides hurting him? I mean, it's not like anyone else knows about this, is it?"

"No one but you." And Bridgett even felt bad about that, but she had known she had to confide in someone about the guilt and confusion she had been feeling, or she would go nuts. And Amy had been the logical choice for a couple of reasons. One, she was the closest thing to a sister Bridgett had, since the two of them had more or less grown up together. Two, Amy was someone she could trust to protect both her and Chase. And three, Amy had weathered some romantic setbacks of her own.

"Do you want me to talk to Chase for you?" Amy asked as she made a final check of the room and found everything in order. "Tell him to back off?"

"No. I can handle it," Bridgett said as she wrote

out a check to Amy's redecorating business. *I can handle him, as long as he doesn't try to kiss me again.* Because if he did and she responded, with even one-tenth the passion she had the last time, and they were somewhere they wouldn't be interrupted when it happened, there was no telling what might occur next.

Amy smiled as she accepted the check and stuffed it into the front of her pastel coveralls. "Okay, well, I hope things work out for you."

"You are coming to my party Saturday night, aren't you?" Bridgett asked as she walked Amy to the door.

Amy hugged her warmly. "I wouldn't miss it for the world."

As soon as Amy had left, Bridgett went back upstairs to get ready for bed. She had just stripped and was liberally applying aloe lotion to her sunburn when the doorbell rang. Bridgett groaned at the interruption and went to the window. Her heartbeat picked up when she saw Chase's Jeep sitting at the curb.

IT TOOK FOREVER for Bridgett to answer the door. Chase even had the idea she was hoping he'd just give up and come back another time. And had Morganstern's Bentley been anywhere around, he probably would have. But since Morganstern didn't seem to be around and it was only nine o'clock, he decided to stick it out and wait for her to answer the doorbell.

Finally she opened the door, and he had to admit it was worth the wait. She looked gorgeous in a two-piece pale-pink lounging-outfit, with a crop top and wide-legged pants that dipped just below her navel. She'd swept her hair off her neck in an untidy knot at the back of her head, but silky wisps escaped to brush her temples, the curve of her cheek and jaw.

"Chase, it's late," she said.

Chase might have felt bad for intruding had he not known that Bridgett was a night owl when she wasn't working, same as he. It would be hours before she went to bed. Deciding not to wait for a formal invitation that might not come, he walked on in as happily as if invited. "I just want to show you the proofs from today."

Bridgett turned sideways to let him pass. As he did so he was inundated with the delicate feminine fragrance of her skin and hair, and a wave of longing swept through him. She smiled at him blissfully, clearly intrigued. "You've got them already?"

"Yeah." Struggling to contain his awareness of her, Chase studied the rosy flush of excess sun across her face and shoulders. Suddenly, his coming by so late did not seem like such a great idea. But he couldn't back away now, because then she'd know something was up with him. Something he wasn't entirely certain either one of them could handle. "Daisy works with a digital camera." Chase swallowed hard around the sudden tightness in his throat as she shut the door behind them, and then ventured even farther into the room. "She downloaded the pictures onto her computer and e-mailed me the proofs this afternoon." Aware he had at last gotten Bridgett's full attention, Chase smiled. "We're a long way from picking the final pictures that will accompany the questions and answers in the magazine, but I thought I'd get your impressions right away. That way if you had any favorite photos, I could make sure we include them," he said kindly. "Before we get to that, though, I wanted to go ahead and do a preliminary draft of our interview. I'll ask the questions. You answer. I'll have hard copy printed up, and we can edit from that."

Abruptly Bridgett looked a lot less cooperative. Maybe because she'd just realized how long all this was going to take. She folded her arms and arched her brow at him skeptically. "You want to do this now?"

Chase nodded, realizing all over again how beautiful and sexy she looked. He shifted his weight to ease the pressure at the front of his slacks. "Unless you've got something better to do."

About a dozen responses flickered in her eyes. To his disappointment, since he was sure they were of the tart-tongued amusing variety, she said none of them aloud. She merely nodded, said, "Fine, then. Let's go upstairs to my private quarters. We'll be more comfortable there than down here in my office.''

Still mulling over her reluctance to engage in repartee with him—because of where a battle of wits and words might lead?—Chase followed Bridgett as she led him through her first-floor office and up the stairs to the second-floor living room. As they walked into the room, Chase blinked in surprise. It looked completely different from the last time he had seen it. ''What happened here?''

''Amy redid it for me.''

No doubt about it, his sister was a decorating genius. And together, Bridgett and Amy had great taste. ''With stuff you already had?''

Bridgett nodded. ''For the most part, although we added a few things.''

''Looks nice.'' Chase said. Cozy. Warm. Pulled together. And yet unpretentious, all at the same time. Very much like Bridgett.

''Thanks.'' Bridgett smiled as she curled up in a corner of the sofa. ''I think your sister did a great job, too.''

He sat down in the wing chair closest to her, unzipped his backpack and got out his tape recorder and notebook. Determined to get their very real business out of the way first before anything of a personal nature, he asked, ''So what's the first step for anyone trying to get his financial affairs in order?''

Bridgett spoke in the direction of his microphone.

"The reader needs to do a complete inventory of all his debts and assets and put it down on paper."

Chase made an unenthusiastic face. "That sounds like a lot of work."

Bridgett shrugged her slender shoulders, the movement of her breasts beneath the soft cotton top telling him she wasn't wearing a bra. "How else are you going to know where you stand—financially, I mean."

"True." Chase tore his eyes from the silky bare skin of her midriff, which was now, thanks to the one-piece swimsuit she'd had on earlier, slightly less tanned than much of the rest of her. No need for him to be thinking just how easy it would be to slide his hands up and underneath that pale pink cropped top of hers. He shifted uncomfortably on the sofa and returned his eyes to her face. He had to stop thinking about making love to her. Going down that road could ruin their friendship. "What do you do when you compile all that information?"

Bridgett looked at him, complete confidence shimmering in her dark-brown eyes, and explained patiently, "You develop a budget that includes both debt repayment and saving, as well as day-to-day expenses."

Chase worked to keep the hoarseness out of his voice. "That sounds even more time-consuming."

Bridgett smirked and shook her head at him. "Are you helping or hindering here?" she asked dryly.

It was Chase's turn to shrug. "I wanted my readers to have something easy."

Bridgett leaned forward earnestly, her belly button—which was a very sexy "inny"—tucking in slightly as she moved. "Saving and investing money can be easy," she told Chase passionately, "but first you have to get organized."

Chase decided if he was going to have even the slightest chance of success here, he needed to get his mind out of the bedroom. Pronto. He swallowed hard and rummaged around in his backpack for some more paper. "Maybe we should make up some charts to help the readers along in the process. Although," he admitted frankly, "I've got to tell you, even though I'd like my readers to save enough of their earnings to be able to afford a place as nice as yours, I don't necessarily think every penny of anyone's paycheck should be accounted for. I think there should be liberal amounts of money for bumming around every month built in to any budget."

Bridgett regarded him skeptically. "Like how much?" she said as she kicked off her sandals and tucked her bare feet beneath her.

"I don't know." Chase shrugged, enjoying their easy banter as much as her decidedly feminine company. He felt his arousal grow as he got another whiff of her perfume. "Twenty-five, fifty percent?" What was the matter with him, anyway? He'd lived in the same house with Bridgett. He'd seen her in sleepwear for years. He'd seen her in a lot less. In bikinis that barely covered the essentials. It had never really bothered him before. Then, he'd barely given her a second look. Now, he couldn't stop looking. Thinking. Considering the *what if*s and the *why shouldn't we*s...

Oblivious to the sexual nature of his thoughts, Bridgett frowned at Chase and leaned toward him impatiently. "Chase, come on. If you advise your readers to blow twenty-five percent of their income on pleasure every month, your readers will never save anything or be able to afford a downpayment on a place of their own."

Chase tore his gaze from the soft movement of her breasts beneath her cotton top. "I'm not saying my readers shouldn't save anything. I think my readers should save something. And I want them to have their own place at the beach or luxury condo or whatever it is they want to own. They just shouldn't put so much money away for the future that they have no funds to have fun in the present."

Bridgett gave him an admonishing look. "You can have fun without spending a lot of money. Take today, for instance. That sea-kayaking expedition didn't cost us anything. And it was a lot of fun."

It had been a lot of fun, Chase admitted. But the idea that it hadn't cost them anything was false. After spending most of the morning and half the afternoon with Bridgett, his peace of mind had gone right out the window. "That's because I owned the kayaks," he murmured, wondering even as he kept up the argument if Bridgett had any idea—even the slightest clue—how very sexy she was. Or did she think men viewed her in the same buttoned-up, way-too-proper way she viewed herself?

"Even if we'd had to rent them—" Bridgett smiled at Chase patiently, once again giving him her full attention "—our expedition to Fort Sumter wouldn't have been all that expensive. Not compared to a dinner at one of the finer restaurants in town, for instance. Which brings me to my next point. As a general principle of ongoing financial savvy, anything that can be done at home, free of charge, like laundry and cleaning and cooking, should be done by the reader. You can save big bucks that way."

Chase stretched his legs out in front of him and leaned back against the sofa cushions, enjoying their give and take more than he'd enjoyed anything in a long time. "That's easy for you to say, you're a girl," he shot back lazily. "My readers are guys. They don't like to do stuff like that."

Bridgett's lips pressed together in a contentious moue. "They should learn," she said emphatically.

"Or get girlfriends or sisters or moms to do it for them," Chase countered mildly.

Bridgett studied him, taking in his short-sleeved madras shirt and olive-green khaki slacks before returning her gaze to his face. "Do the females in your life do your domestic chores?"

Chase knew a loaded question when he heard

one. "No," he admitted frankly, studying the blush of too much sun on Bridgett's face and the unabashed interest in her eyes. "But that's just because I don't want them underfoot."

"So you do them," Bridgett said, a new edge in her voice.

Chase wondered if he was ever going to figure out a way to impress her to the degree he suddenly wanted to impress her, while still being himself. "I keep my place neat enough, but I draw the line at laundry."

She shook her head, still holding his gaze. Chase felt his pulse kick up another notch. "Let me guess. You don't approve of me sending my clothes out?"

"Honestly? I think you're wasting money, big time."

Chase inclined his head slightly to the side and narrowed his eyes at her. "I suppose you do all yours?" For some reason that seemed sexy to him, too. In fact, there wasn't anything he could think of about her right now that didn't seem sexy.

"I used to." Bridgett leaned back and stretched, abruptly looking and acting as physically restless as he felt. "Now, most of what I wear has to be dry-cleaned."

"Then our laundry bills are probably the same, 'cause all my stuff is wash-and-wear."

She conceded his point, reluctantly, and they spent the next fifteen minutes talking about various investment strategies, going over the difference between stocks and mutual funds, municipals bonds and the various types of individual retirement accounts. Chase was impressed but not surprised that she not only knew her stuff, but could explain it in down-to-earth terms. By the time they had finished and he had tailored her advice just for guys, he knew his readers were going to get a lot out of the article.

"That was easy enough," she said, looking as relieved as he was that business was over.

"This will be, too," Chase promised as he got his laptop out of his backpack and, for lack of a better place, put it on the coffee table in front of the sofa. He opened it up, turned it on and accessed the photos. Bridgett moved close enough to see the screen. He picked up the laptop and situated the computer so it was half on his thigh, half on hers. "Here's where we started," he said, already wondering if Bridgett was going to get the same kick in the gut he had when he had first viewed the pictures of the morning's outing.

He scrolled through the hundred or so photos Daisy had taken. Bridgett looked at them in silence, one after another, gazing at the raw intimacy Daisy had managed to capture on film. An intimacy that went way beyond two old childhood friends and seemed to indicate a blossoming—forbidden—love affair. Finally, when she'd come to the end of them, Bridgett shook her head and sighed her displeasure.

"We can't use any of these photos, Chase," she said crisply.

Chase looked at her in stunned amazement. "Why the heck not?"

"Because," Bridgett said before vaulting up and off the sofa, "those photos of us look like..."

"What?" Chase demanded when she didn't finish.

"Well, they're misleading." Arms folded tightly in front of her, Bridgett began to pace.

"Misleading how?" Chase asked, holding her gaze and playing dumb. He wanted to hear her say it.

"The way we're looking at each other here..." Bridgett sat back down beside him, took the laptop computer entirely onto her lap and scrolled back to the series of photos taken on the observation deck at Fort Sumter, just before they'd been inundated with schoolchildren on a field trip. "We don't look like friends here," she pointed out unhappily.

Chase looked at the enamored expressions on their faces, recalling full well how they had been about to kiss and would have, had they not been interrupted. "We look like lovers," he said softly, wanting her to face what was happening between them, too.

"But we're not lovers," Bridgett protested hotly. She shoved the computer at him and vaulted from the sofa again.

But we want to be, unless I am misreading all the

signals you are sending me, Chase thought as he watched her resume pacing the small room in agitation. For the first time he allowed himself to wonder if they could be lovers *and* friends. Not just for a while, but for the long haul. Knowing he had never enjoyed a woman's company more, Chase set his laptop computer carefully on the coffee table out of harm's way. "The camera doesn't lie, Bridgett," Chase said quietly.

"In this case, I think it does." Her shoulders tensing even more, Bridgett walked to the French doors and opened them onto the piazza.

"Are you sure about that?" Chase stood, too. He crossed to her side and forced her to face him. "Because I think what's in those pictures is already in your heart. And mine. Face it, Bridgett. There's no way in hell you should be looking at me like that if you're going to marry Morganstern." There was no way they could continue to pretend the chemistry between them didn't exist.

Bridgett pushed him away and stalked out onto the moonlit piazza, where the scent of honeysuckle and magnolia blossoms filled the night air. "Then what should I do?" she cried as she crossed to the edge of the covered porch and put her arm around one of the thick white pillars that supported the roof above her. "Have a fling with you? Because that's all it would ever be, Chase. A fling."

He noticed she had stopped denying she desired him. That was a start, anyway, to dealing honestly with whatever this was between them. "Flings end. I don't see this ending."

"Did you see your relationship with Maggie ending when you got involved with her?" Bridgett asked in a low serious voice.

Chase stared at Bridgett in frustration. She was deliberately misconstruing events and she knew it. "That was different," he stated firmly.

Bridgett turned to face him and stood with her back to the round white column. "Different, how?"

"Because I thought at that time that I wanted to get married and settle down, and I was looking for a wife. Maggie seemed to be everything I wanted in a spouse—sweet, kind, undemanding, supportive."

"Your basic helpmate."

"I guess."

Silence fell between them as Bridgett moved back toward the yellow light spilling from the doorway of her living room. Disappointment glimmered in her eyes as she turned and regarded him quietly. "Did you love her?"

"In retrospect, probably not," Chase admitted, disillusionment filling his heart. "But at the time, it felt perfect."

"Only, it couldn't have been." Bridgett tilted her chin at him stubbornly. "She couldn't have loved you, either. Otherwise, your relationship with Maggie never would have ended the way it did."

"Maggie said she loved me, but for me it was

only infatuation, the thrill of the hunt. Once we were ready to walk down the aisle, my infatuation with her ended. She said I was never meant to get married, that I only wanted the challenge of getting a woman to say yes.''

Bridgett shot him an ominous look. "Is that true?"

"To a point, yeah," Chase conceded reasonably. "Marriage scares the hell out of me. The thought of making promises I might not be able to keep, well…" He paused, shook his head. "It's just not something I really want to do."

Bridgett's eyes widened. "Ever?" she questioned, aghast.

Chase shrugged helplessly, caring about Bridgett too much to lie to her. "I'm just not sure marriage is a workable institution. Maybe people are just supposed to be together as long as they make each other happy. Maybe the idea of being together for a lifetime is just not a workable concept in this day and age."

Bridgett sighed and folded her arms. "How do you figure that?"

Chase lifted both hands, palms up. "Look at our own families. Any distress your mother had was caused by wanting your biological father to marry her. When that yearning stopped, so did her suffering. My aunt Winnifred still hasn't recovered from being widowed a year after saying her vows. The hurt my parents inflicted on each other in their divorce is legendary. The same goes for my brother Mitch's situation—his divorce was so ugly people are still talking about it.''

"Next you'll be talking about the Deveraux curse,'' Bridgett muttered disparagingly.

"No,'' Chase said, not about to let Bridgett bully him into taking back his sentiments on the subject. ''The hurt marriage can dish out is much more far-reaching than that. The hurt marriage inflicts on people involves everyone who even tries it.''

Bridgett studied Chase, her expression suddenly becoming closed and unreadable again. ''How did Gabe figure in what happened between you and Maggie?'' she asked casually, leading the way back into her living room.

"I don't know.'' Chase followed her, taking in the graceful sway of her hips. ''I never gave him a chance to explain.''

Bridgett whirled to face him. ''Why not?'' she demanded impatiently.

Because I didn't want to hear it. ''I caught my fiancée looking at my brother like he just hung the moon. And when I asked her if she was attracted to him, she didn't even try to deny it. What else was there to say?'' Chase challenged.

Bridgett released an exasperated breath. ''Plenty, maybe, if you'd ever given Gabe a chance,'' she said.

Chase paused. He studied the flushed contours of

her upturned face. ''You think I should hear his side of things, do you?''

Bridgett nodded, her dark eyes lasering into his in a way that let him know she had always thought that. ''For the sake of family unity,'' she said quietly, ''yes, Chase, I do.''

CHASE FOUND GABE at the hospital in the doctor's lounge. He didn't look any happier to see Chase than Chase was to see him. ''If you're here to punch me out again,'' Gabe said dryly, ''beware. The hospital has a policy against biting the hands that heal.''

Chase released a long breath and jammed his hands on his waist. He was glad he'd been able to track Gabe down so quickly and they had the chance to talk alone. Bridgett was right—this had been a long time coming. ''I don't intend to hit you,'' he said.

Gabe dropped onto one of the sofas in the room and sent Chase a grin that brought forth memories of other brawls the two of them had gotten into while growing up. Punching hadn't always been involved, true, but the two of them had usually ended up rolling around on the floor or breaking something, anyway, during the scuffle. ''That's good,'' Gabe said, '''cause then I'd have to slug you back. And hospital security would be in here in no time flat to haul us both away.''

Recalling what Bridgett had said to him about giving his brother a chance to tell his side of the story, Chase shoved his hands into the pockets of his slacks and said, "I never gave you a chance to explain what happened."

"Are you willing to listen now?" Gabe's voice turned contentious.

Chase shrugged, even as he warned himself to hang on to his temper. "That's why I'm here," he said.

Gabe continued to regard Chase with stony resolve a moment longer, then said, "The week of the wedding, I saw that Maggie had some doubts."

"About marrying me," Chase guessed, knowing that of all the guys he knew, Gabe was the most intuitive when it came to women. He seemed to understand them in a way most men didn't. Chase envied him that ability, even as he resented what Gabe had done.

Gabe nodded reluctantly. "At first, I took her aside and tried to talk her out of it. I told her what a great husband you'd make, but she said the closer the two of you got to the wedding, the more distant and distracted you'd become, to the point you barely seemed to know she was alive. She wanted out, but you know how she is."

Chase remembered. "She's not the kind of woman to make waves."

"And her father had already spent a fortune trying to put on a wedding they could ill afford, and most of the deposits were nonrefundable."

Chase scowled. "I would have paid those."

"Her father never would have allowed it. And she knew it."

Chase paused. He was beginning to feel as if he should forgive Gabe, even though he didn't want to. "She told me she had feelings for you," he said.

Gabe shrugged. "I don't deny there was some chemistry." He looked Chase straight in the eye. "But I never slept with her."

Chase believed him—about that. "What about the other day at the beach house?" he demanded gruffly, suddenly wanting this unpleasantness to be over between him and Gabe.

"She needed a favor from me on a medical matter. I turned her down. I told her things were still dicey enough between you and me already without making them worse."

Made sense, Chase admitted reluctantly, since Maggie had always trusted Gabe's judgment on medical matters implicitly, even when Gabe had still been a resident physician undergoing training. "And the kiss I saw?" Chase barked.

"Was simply goodbye," Gabe said.

Which meant one thing, Chase thought. Bridgett had been right all along.

Chapter Eleven

Chase was halfway out the door to his beach house the next morning when his brother Mitch drove up. Looking as impeccably groomed and buttoned-up as always in his suit and tie, Mitch climbed out of his Jaguar and said, "Mom asked me to tell you we're having a family dinner tonight at the house. She's cooking and she wants us all there."

"Mom's cooking?" Chase was stunned. Everyone knew his mother didn't know how to cook. Not at all. And she certainly hadn't had time to take those lessons she'd been wanting.

Mitch nodded. "Mom gave Theresa the night off so Theresa could plan the party for Bridgett."

Chase swore. This was all he needed. His mother trying gaily to pretend nothing was wrong when something clearly was. His father on edge—probably because he hadn't yet figured out how to behave at family affairs in the wake of the divorce he had never wanted. And he and Gabe still not exactly friends.

Mitch read his mind and warned, "Just show up and be nice. I don't care what Gabe and Maggie Callaway have been up to, then or now. No more fights with Gabe."

Chase finished locking up and walked down the steps. "You don't have to worry about that," he said serenely. "Gabe and I made our peace."

Mitch's jaw dropped in stunned amazement. "When?"

"Last night." Briefly Chase explained. "So if that's all…" He continued past Mitch, in a hurry to get to Harlan Decker's office.

"It's not."

Chase turned and waited.

Mitch's frown deepened. "Amy told me you've been putting the moves on Bridgett."

Chase tensed. He should have known he couldn't keep anything secret from his family. "How does she know that?" he bit out.

"So you're not denying it," Mitch surmised unhappily.

Chase took exception to the censure in his brother's low voice. "What happened or didn't happen is between Bridgett and me," he stated heatedly.

"Listen to me, Chase." Mitch put on his sunglasses and clamped his lips together. "I don't want to see Bridgett hurt. Neither does Amy."

"I'm not going to hurt Bridgett!" Chase snapped, losing his cool. She was his best friend in the whole world. He would lay down his life for her! "Besides, Amy doesn't want Bridgett to marry Martin any more than I do."

"Amy also knows, just as I do, that it's not our decision to make. It's Bridgett's."

Chase knew his brother was a genius when it came to the shipping business that had supported the Deveraux clan in style for nearly two hundred years, but Mitch was hardly an expert on women and love. Mitch's extremely unpleasant divorce two years back had proved that. "Martin Morganstern won't make her happy," Chase reiterated bluntly, aware he and his brother Gabe were equally bad at dealing with the opposite sex. Gabe could get a woman to turn to him for help and Chase could attract them, but none of them could hold onto a woman for any length of time or forge a real and lasting relationship. "And frankly, I can't understand why Bridgett thinks, even for one minute, that he will. The man has no real passion for anything but the good life and the art in his gallery."

"Yeah, well, you see, there's your problem," Mitch parried, adopting a lighter but no less goading tone. "Passion will get you in trouble every time."

Chase knew Mitch felt that everything, including a person's personal life, should be run with the efficiency of the Deveraux finance department. But business didn't keep a person warm at night. Business could only satisfy a person so far. Chase wanted more out of life. So should Mitch. And Bridgett.

Chase slipped on his sunglasses, too. "Passion," Chase corrected, "is the only thing worth living for." To exist without it, well…he didn't want even to contemplate that. And neither should Bridgett.

"SO WHAT HAVE YOU got on Morganstern?" Chase asked the moment he was in the private investigator's office door.

"Nothing that will cause this gal to call off the wedding," Harlan said. "He's squeaky clean."

Chase forced himself to remain calm as he eased into a chair in front of Harlan's desk. "He can't be." Chase had a pretty good gut instinct about these things. That instinct was telling him that ol' Martin was not the right guy for Bridgett, for reasons that weren't easily visible to the naked eye. He had been counting on Decker to uncover what precisely those flaws were.

"Sorry, kid. At least, according to the facts, he is above reproach. His art gallery isn't making a ton of money, thanks to the number of up-and-coming artists he sponsors, but it is revered throughout the Southeast. He invests judiciously, so the family fortune is intact—which means there's no reason for him to be marrying that gal for the money she's made with her writing."

Chase gripped the arms of the chair he was sitting

in. "What about his history with women?" he demanded.

Harlan shrugged. "He's dated a number of women through the years, but the scuttlebutt around the garden clubs in town is that the woman always broke off the relationship. Mainly because he wasn't interested in marriage."

"Until now," Chase concluded grimly.

"With that gal friend of yours, yeah." Harlan pulled out a cigar and lit the end of it. "He wants kids now, though, so that's probably what's changed his mind about heading down the aisle."

Bridgett wanted kids, too.

The PI sat back in his chair and blew smoke rings above his head. "That happens to a lot of confirmed bachelors when they hit their forties. They realize time is getting away from them. And it's a now-or-never proposition."

Chase sighed. He had been so sure Harlan would find something he could use. He looked the street-smart detective square in the eye. "There's nothing I could tell Bridgett that might change her mind about marrying Morganstern?" he asked, more aware than ever that time was running out.

Harlan shook his head, "The guy has never gotten so much as a traffic ticket. And he really knows how to treat a lady."

"There's more to life than good manners," Chase argued. Good manners alone were not going to make Bridgett happy for the rest of her life.

"That may be, but the ladies really go for his charm and sophistication." Harlan regarded Chase sympathetically. Apparently not about to pull any punches, he continued, "I think you're out of luck."

Not necessarily, Chase thought, his mind already leaping ahead to the next possibility. He wasn't giving up until the last dog died. "What about her father?" he asked impatiently, knowing he still had one ace left up his sleeve. "Were you able to locate him?"

Harlan nodded. He scribbled down an address and phone number and slid them over to Chase. "He still owns the textile mill in Greenville he inherited years ago from his folks."

"THERE'S NO WAY on this green earth that I'm going to let you extort money out of me," Simon Oglethorpe told Chase the moment he was ushered into the well-appointed library at his country estate just outside of Greenville. "And to make sure of that, I've asked my lawyer to be here with us for this meeting."

Chase had no idea what kind of man Simon had been in his youth, but he could see what the man was now. He was a suspicious, nasty blue blood with none of the warmth or love in him that a woman like Bridgett deserved from a parent.

"Furthermore—" Simon narrowed his icy eyes at Chase through the lenses of his small gold-framed glasses "—I categorically deny being that young woman's father!"

Chase took in the man's jodhpurs, silk shirt and ascot and wondered if he thought he was living in colonial Africa, instead of at the foot of the Blue Ridge Mountains. "Theresa Owens wouldn't lie."

"Well, apparently Theresa has." Simon stalked the length of the library in his knee-high boots. He paused beneath a stuffed shark, displayed above the mantel. "And I told that to her daughter the last time she was here."

This was something Harlan Decker hadn't uncovered. Chase inhaled slowly. "Bridgett was here to see you?"

Simon nodded. He stalked back to his desk and sat down in the imposing leather chair behind it. "Ten years ago, on her twenty-second birthday. I told her then her mother had obviously misled her and I asked her not to ever bother me again."

"You said that to her face," Chase ascertained, struggling to remain in his chair. He was getting a powerful urge to punch the guy.

"Yes." Simon gave Chase a tight-lipped smile and pushed his glasses closer to his eyes. "Fortunately she believed me and left. Which, by the way, is exactly what you should do."

Chase ignored the hint. For the life of him he couldn't see one decent thing in this guy who had sired Bridgett, but for her sake, he had to try to get through the defenses to the kinder, gentler person he hoped was somewhere beneath the haughty disdain and mega-attitude. "How can you do this to Bridgett?" Chase asked in the same low, conscience-prodding tone his own parents had used on him many times. "How can you hurt her that way?"

Simon Oglethorpe looked at his lawyer. The lawyer nodded. Simon turned back to Chase and stood, signaling the meeting was over, whether Chase liked it or not. "Look, son, I have a family. Children. That's all I need."

And Bridgett, her mother and what they had been through because of this man's selfish irresponsibility be damned, Chase added silently.

"I don't want trouble here," Simon continued as he showed Chase the door. "But I promise you, if you or that young woman ever come and darken my doorstep again," Simon concluded grimly, "it's trouble you're going to get."

CHASE HEARD his mother's soft melodious laugh floating out through the open kitchen windows. Wondering what had prompted her amusement, he opened the door and walked in, then blinked in shock at what he saw. His mother standing very close to his father. The pair of them talking in hushed tones—hushed *flirtatious* tones. And it looked to him as if his father wanted very much to kiss his mother, and vice versa.

Chase felt a flare of hope, then warned himself not to jump to conclusions. He had wanted his parents to reconcile for a long time, even though it had never looked as if this would happen. Yes, his father had agreed to stay at the mansion along with his mother this time, instead of bunking at a hotel as usual. But that was only because his mother was planning to be at the house for several weeks, instead of the usual day or so. The two were bedding down at opposite ends of the upstairs hall, leading their own very separate lives. Still, there was something going on here. Something new. Different. And he hated to interrupt.

He was about to retreat and go out in as unnoticed a manner as he had come in when Grace turned and saw him. "Chase!" Grace blushed and backed away from Tom immediately, and went back to stirring whatever it was she was cooking on the stove. "You're the first to arrive." She stirred so hard sauce glopped up over the side of the pan.

Hoping they wouldn't notice how bummed out he was about not being able to reunite Bridgett with her father and hence, put a stop to whatever plans she had to spend the rest of her life with a man who was nothing but a father figure, Chase merely smiled and asked, "What's for dinner?"

"Garlic-roasted chicken and scalloped potatoes, peas and salad." Grace tried to wipe up the excess mess around one of the burners, and the end of her dish towel nearly caught on fire. "I'm making the white sauce now," she said as she hastily carried the smoking cloth to the sink to dampen under running water. "And your father has graciously agreed to peel the potatoes for me."

Chase looked at his dad in astonishment. He'd never known his father to do anything in the kitchen, period. But here he was, tie off, shirtsleeves rolled up above his elbows, slowly and clumsily wielding a knife. His mother must have exercised some influence. Either that, or Tom was simply working hard to get in Grace's favor.

"I tried to catch you at your office earlier," Tom said. "They said you were out until Monday."

Chase had an idea how that played with his never-missed-a-day-of-work-if-I-could-help-it-and-I-usually-could father. He went to the refrigerator and helped himself to an ice-cold beer. Bypassing the opportunity to explain how he always took a few days off after putting a month of his magazine to bed, Chase merely shrugged and said, "I had something important to do."

Grace slanted him an inquisitive glance, but as always was too discreet to pry.

Chase knew he could say nothing more and neither parent would press the issue. But he also figured he needed to confide in someone who'd had children, who could help him make sense of what he'd uncovered. "I went to see Bridgett's father."

Tom put down his knife and stared at Chase. "That's why you wanted the name of a PI," he said.

Chase nodded. "I figured maybe if Bridgett had a relationship with her dad, she wouldn't be so hell-bent on marrying that geezer. But it didn't work out the way I had hoped.'' Briefly Chase filled his parents in on the details, then said, ''I just can't understand why Simon Oglethorpe would refuse to acknowledge Bridgett.''

''He told you,'' Tom said patiently, ''that he already has a wife and family to tend to.''

A vaguely irked expression on her face, Grace began tearing the lettuce into bite-size pieces.

''He has a responsibility to Bridgett, too,'' Chase argued back as he uncapped his beer and took a swig.

Tom shrugged and began slicing the potato he'd just peeled. ''Maybe he's meeting it in other ways,'' he said.

''Such as...?'' Chase was surprised his dad would take Simon Oglethorpe's side on this, when his dad had always been so devoted to his own children. ''We know he never supported Bridgett financially. If he won't acknowledge her personally or be there for her emotionally, what other ways are there?''

Tom clamped his lips together in obvious frustration. ''Look, it's just not always as simple as it seems. I'm sure Simon has his reasons. And who knows, maybe Bridgett is better off without Simon Oglethorpe in her life.''

''I don't know how you can say that when she's about to throw her life away by marrying some old geezer,'' Chase retorted heatedly.

Again his mother remained silent. Chase watched her tear the lettuce angrily. "What do you think about this?" Chase asked her finally. It wasn't like her not to weigh in when it came to family dilemmas, and Theresa and Bridgett were both considered family.

Grace stared grimly at the tile back-splash above the stove. "I think men who have families shouldn't sire children with women other than their wives, that's what I think!" she said vehemently.

Chase knew his mother cared about Bridgett and Theresa—all the Deveraux did. But her protectiveness seemed to go beyond that. "So what do you think I should do?" Chase asked his mother cautiously after a moment.

In the end, it was Tom who answered him. "Leave well enough alone, son," Tom advised sternly.

Grace gave the simmering white sauce another stir. "So what else have you been up to?" she asked Chase in her best let's-change-the-subject-for-all-our-sakes tone.

Deciding maybe his mother was right, Chase leaned against the counter and took another swig of his beer. "I talked Bridgett into letting me feature her in *Modern Man.* I did an interview with her last night, and we also did a photo essay yesterday." Briefly Chase explained about the sea-kayaking expedition to Fort Sumter. "I asked Daisy Templeton to take the pictures."

Looking tenser than ever, Grace consulted a recipe and began layering potato slices in the bottom of a buttered casserole dish. "I thought Daisy was still a college student."

"She got kicked out of Wellesley a few weeks ago, so she's back in Charleston again. To tell you the truth, I don't know if she'll ever graduate, but she's one heck of a photographer. She takes photos that are just incredible in their truth," Chase said, thinking of the way Daisy'd captured Bridgett looking at him on film—as if Bridgett wanted him in her life, and in her bed.

"I'm not sure Daisy's family would want you taking advantage of her that way," Tom said as the white sauce on the stove bubbled up higher.

"Hey, I'm paying her exactly what I pay every photographer I hire for my magazine," Chase said in his own defense. Though what it was to his father, he didn't know, since—to his observation, anyway—the Templetons and the Deveraux weren't all that close.

Grace's cheeks took on a pink tint. "I think what your father is trying to say is that your giving Daisy a job now might prevent her from being motivated to go back to college and finish." Grace looked at Chase sternly. "I wouldn't want you to be responsible for ruining Daisy's life. She's obviously had a very hard time as it is."

Now Tom looked angry. Why, Chase couldn't figure.

"I think we should drop this whole subject," Tom said curtly, turning to Chase as a peculiar unappetizing flavor rose from the saucepan on the stove. "Let Bridgett handle her own life and make her own decisions," he said. "And for pity's sake, don't mention anything about this to Theresa!"

"I agree," Grace said tensely as the unpleasant smell in the room grew stronger and stronger. She shook a spoon covered with gloppy white stuff at Chase. "Once something's done, it's done, and whether you like it or not, you can't go back and change Bridgett's paternity. All you can do by bringing it up is embarrass Bridgett and her mother, and I will not have either Bridgett or Theresa humiliated that way!"

Chase wrinkled his nose. "Is it my imagination or is something burning?" he asked.

Grace rushed back to the stove. The white sauce had turned a funny brown color and was bubbling almost over the top of the pan. She cried out in dismay and turned off the element.

UNFORTUNATELY FOR THEM ALL, dinner went the way of the white sauce and was, if not totally inedible, not very tasty. Worse, his mother and father were barely speaking to each other, for reasons Chase couldn't fathom.

Not that this was the first time the two of them had gone from warm to cold in a matter of minutes. They'd been like that a lot both before and after their divorce. Chase could tell his mother resented the heck out of his father and still blamed him for something he'd done or hadn't done. And his dad was equally frustrated with his mother. Chase figured it all went back to the mysterious reasons for their divorce.

Hence, Chase got out of there as soon as he could. And the minute he got back to his beach house that night, he reached for the bicarbonate of soda. He had just fixed himself a tall glass of the soothing concoction when he heard a car engine outside. He glanced out the window and felt a mixture of anticipation and dread as he saw Bridgett charging across the sand and up the steps. She was furious, he noted. And from the looks of it, probably with him.

Chapter Twelve

Chase wondered if Bridgett had any idea how beautiful she looked charging toward him in the moonlight, the waves crashing against the sandy white beach forming a romantic backdrop. His immediate neighbors had already gone to bed, and the only real light where he was standing was the soft glow of the lanterns on the perimeter of his deck.

"I don't believe you!" Bridgett said as she stormed up the wide wooden steps to confront him. Her auburn hair tumbled over her shoulders in loose flowing curls. She was dressed in a snug black cocktail dress that outlined her every curve to a tantalizing degree and at the same time comically restricted her stride to little more than baby steps. High-heeled black sandals and sheer black stockings made the most of her sensational legs.

Watching her, Chase couldn't help but grin, even as his lower half sprang to life. Who would have thought Bridgett would be doing the sexpot walk? He bet she hadn't considered how hard it would be to march anywhere quickly in that narrow-hemmed dress when she'd purchased it.

"Who told you that you could meddle in my life!" Bridgett said as she closed the remaining distance between them with short, hip-swiveling steps.

Chase tore his eyes from the sexy fit of her dress around her slender thighs and cute-as-buttons knees and concentrated on the very big trouble he was definitely in. He supposed this was what he got for trying to help his very best friend in the whole world. Slowly he let his gaze rove her upturned face, lingering on the pert tilt of her nose and the softness of her lips before returning to her eyes. "How'd you find out?" he asked, already wondering just what it was going to take to get her to forgive him.

"I read this!" Bridgett slapped a piece of paper in his hand.

Chase studied the fax transmission. It was from Simon Oglethorpe's lawyer and had been sent to Bridgett's home. The letter warned her she would be facing harassment charges if she or Chase ever bothered him again.

Chase stared at it in frustration. The last thing he had wanted was to cause more grief for Bridgett, who in his estimation, had been hurt more than enough by her father's abandonment. Chase felt his gut tighten. Sorrow inundated his low voice as he looked at her again and reluctantly explained, "I was trying to help."

Without warning, moisture shimmered in her

eyes. Bridgett looked as if she wanted to punch something—namely, him. Her lower lip trembled as she demanded emotionally, "By going behind my back?"

"By bringing your father back into your life," Chase corrected as he caught and held her gaze, beginning to get upset at how quick she was to try and convict him. He set the paper onto the stylish wrought-iron table beside him and put an unlit citronella candle on top of it so it wouldn't blow away in the evening breeze. He turned back to her and took another step toward her, wanting the new tension between them to disappear as quickly as it had sprung up. "I had no idea you'd ever been to see him." Unable to quell his hurt, he tightened his lips with a mixture of hurt and displeasure. "You never said anything to me."

The tears she had been holding back rolled down her cheeks. Bridgett dashed them away with the back of her hand. "I never said anything to anyone about what happened that day, not even my mother," she replied in a strangled voice.

Chase thought about what a hard secret that must have been to keep. Once again he wished he could have been there for her in the way she had obviously needed him to be. "So your mom doesn't know you met Simon Oglethorpe," Chase said softly.

"I didn't want to hurt her." Strain reverberated in the low note of her voice. "It was bad enough, the way the louse rejected her after she got pregnant.''

Deciding she needed to sit down, Chase took her hand and led her to a chaise. When she was sitting back against the thick green-and-white-striped cushions, he sat down in another right beside her, facing her, still holding one of her hands in both of his. ''Do you know what happened between them?''

Bridgett drew a deep trembling breath. Suddenly, it seemed, she needed to confide in him, every bit as much as he needed to hear it.

''They met when my mom was nineteen. She was waiting tables at a place out on the beach.'' Bitterness and hurt crept into Bridgett's low tone as some of the tension left her shoulders and she turned her hand palm up to mesh her fingers with his. ''Oglethorpe was there with his family.'' She dropped her gaze to her lap. ''He romanced her like she'd never been romanced before, made her believe he was in love with her and would marry her as soon as he'd finished college. She believed him.''

Chase sighed. He wished he could erase all the unhappiness of the past. Let everyone live happily ever after without all this heartbreak and angst. ''Until your mother got pregnant and found out otherwise,'' he guessed.

Bridgett nodded, her lower lip trembling once again with the effort it was costing her to hold back her emotions and continue in a flat, matter-of-fact tone. "He wanted her to terminate the pregnancy. When my mom wouldn't, well, that was it."

What a bastard, Chase thought. No wonder Theresa was worried about her daughter. No wonder Bridgett also found it so hard to trust.

Chase studied Bridgett's face. "Why didn't your mother go after him for child support?" he asked, trying to understand how Theresa, who was also a very strong woman in her own right, let Simon ignore his financial responsibilities to his child.

Bridgett stood, restless again, and paced away from him to the waist-high wooden railing that edged the deck. She leaned against it, her hands clasped in front of her, elbows resting on the rail, auburn hair blowing in the wind. Wanting only to be as close to her as it was possible to get, Chase got up and followed her wordlessly.

Bridgett turned to face him, one forearm still on the railing. She looked up into his eyes. "He said if my mother tried—if she forced him to pay— there'd be a custody fight over me and he'd win. With his family connections and money, my mother knew he'd probably get at least partial custody and she was afraid of what being put in an environment where I would be resented, instead of loved, might do to me. So she told him what he wanted to hear— that I wasn't his baby, after all, and they never saw each other or had any contact again."

Chase moved closer to her. He breathed in the jonquil and vanilla fragrance of her skin and hair.

"I'm sorry," he said sadly, wishing he could do something to erase all the unhappiness she had suffered and was still dealing with. "I wish things had been different for you, growing up."

Bridgett stiffened. The don't-you-dare-pity-me look was back in her eyes. "I had a fine childhood, Chase."

Chase had never admired her spunk, her inner toughness, more than he did at that moment. "In a lot of ways, yeah, you did," Chase agreed as he caught the strand of hair blowing across her face and gently tucked it behind her ear. Whether she wanted to or not, he figured it was time they talked about this openly and honestly. He looked deeply into her eyes. "But you also missed having a dad."

Bridgett shrugged indifferently and cut him off with a defiant glance. "Fortunately," she said, the softness in her low voice at odds with the terrier-toughness in her attitude, "I had your dad watching out for me."

Chase regarded her with more tenderness than he had ever thought himself capable of. "Unfortunately it wasn't enough," Chase said. "Otherwise…"

Bridgett's soft lower lip shot out in a truculent manner before he could finish. Chase knew that look. It was the look that said she wasn't going to let anyone close to her. "Otherwise what?" she demanded impatiently.

"Otherwise, you wouldn't be about to make the

mistake of your life, by entering into what you and I and everyone else in Charleston know is going to be a loveless marriage!'' Chase shot right back.

Bridgett glared at him and stepped back a pace. She folded her arms beneath her breasts, the action pushing the uppermost curves out of the sexy V neckline of her dress. ''And you, Mr. Bachelor-of-the-decade, think you're qualified to judge,'' she taunted.

''I know I am,'' Chase said hotly.

Her pretty chin went up a notch and fire ignited in her eyes. ''On what basis?''

On the only one that mattered, Chase thought. ''On the basis I care about you,'' he said, closing the distance between them in one swift determined stride.

''Care?'' Bridgett echoed hoarsely as he pulled her into his arms.

''Yes, care!'' Chase declared.

He told himself it was just to shut her up, but even as he brought her closer yet, so they were touching the full length of their bodies and his lips found hers, he knew it was a heck of a lot more than that. He had wanted Bridgett forever. In his arms. Kissing him. Just like this. He rubbed his lips across hers, gently at first, then with growing intensity. He let his hand slide through her hair to the back of her neck, and the way she melted against him then, all soft and wanting, made his heart pound. He wanted her, just like this. And though he knew there would be hell to pay later for what he was about to do, right now he didn't care.

She groaned as his tongue found its way into her mouth and tangled with hers. "Chase…"

He knew all the reasons they shouldn't be together, even as he felt the desire pouring from them both. He also knew none of those reasons mattered anymore, if indeed they ever had.

Determined to make Bridgett see what she would be missing if she pledged herself to another man, a man who was all wrong for her, Chase tucked his thumbs beneath her chin and angled her mouth, for better access. Her lips were soft and hot and yielding beneath his, and so was her body. Pouring everything he felt, everything he wanted and needed into the embrace, he kissed her again and again, until whatever reservations she might have had fled and she was kissing him back with all the fervor she possessed. His body throbbed and heated and demanded more. Much more. But it wasn't going to be out here on the deck, he thought fiercely. It was going to be upstairs. In his bed.

Still kissing her, he danced her backward toward the door, one hot passionate caress melting into another. When they stepped inside, his impatience to make her his won out over the pressing need to have her lips beneath his. Aware he was already hard as a rock and they hadn't even caressed each other yet, he kept one arm around her shoulders and slid the other beneath her knees. She had a dazed yearning look in her eyes as he carried her up the stairs to his loft.

He put her down next to the bed. Her eyes widened. She looked wary again. Caution had gotten the better of them for too long. Too much caution was what had led them both to nearly marry the wrong person. No more, Chase thought as he brushed his thumb across her lower lip. Not when they had the chance to discover what it was they really wanted, needed. He brought her other hand to his mouth and pressed a kiss to the back of her knuckles. The kiss was both harder and sweeter than he'd intended. He wanted Bridgett to feel as overwhelmed as he did by what was happening between them. He wanted her to feel the power of their attraction for each other, the need. He wanted her to throw caution to the wind and make love with him.

His satisfaction deepened as Bridgett released a sigh and wrapped both her hands around his neck. He felt the soft surrender of her body pressing against his, the hot sweetness of her lips. This, Chase realized belatedly, was all he had ever wanted. Bridgett was all he had ever wanted.

Still holding her close, Chase kissed her until she arched against him and her breaths were as short and shallow as his. For so long he had been restless, filled with yearning. Now, at last, he knew why. The two of them were destined to be together. To make love together and feel and experience everything possible.

Needing, wanting, more, he slipped his hand inside the neckline of her dress and smoothed his hand from the silk of her shoulder to the silk of her breast, spilling out of her bra. She trembled in response, her flesh swelling to fill his palm. He pushed the fabric aside until he could cup the full weight of her breast in his palm. Bridgett gasped and swayed as his lips traced the path his hand had taken. Her nipple budded in his mouth, even as his hands slid beneath the hem of her dress, along the soft insides of her thighs. "Chase..."

Her whimpered plea was all the encouragement he needed to take their lovemaking another step. The dress had to come off, he thought as he unzipped the garment, feathered kisses down her neck, across the top of her breasts. He pushed the fabric down her hips, let it fall to the floor in a circle around her feet. Then he unhooked the lacy black bra and tugged everything else off. She was even more beautiful than he had imagined. He gently caressed the mounds of creamy flesh with his palms, savoring the silky warmth and softness of her skin, then bent his head and took a rosy nipple into his mouth, sucking lightly on the tender bud. Bridgett drew in a quick urgent breath, then wove her hands through his hair, holding him close. He loved her with his mouth and hands and tongue until her back arched and her knees faltered and he had no choice but to lower her to the bed.

"Oh, Chase," she whispered, bringing him closer

yet as he shucked his own clothes and stretched out beside her. She looked at him, her eyes glowing with desire. ''If this is what it's going to be like between us, I don't want to wait.''

''Neither do I,'' Chase murmured back, his heart filling with wonder that she was really here with him like this, in his bed. ''Neither do I.'' As he felt the increasing hunger in her body, everything blurred and all rational thought flew from his mind. The jonquil and vanilla scent of her filling his senses, Chase kissed his way across the tan lines, past her sexy navel and the perfection of her abdomen, to the warm moistness beneath. She stretched sinuously and melted against him, her hands curling around his shoulders as he found his way to the silken core of her. She tasted as sweet and delicate as he had hoped, and she moaned soft and low in her throat and arched her head back even more. Her passionate response, coupled with the urgent press of her hands on his shoulders, sent need throbbing to his groin. ''Now, Chase,'' she said. She grabbed his upper arms, her fingers digging into his biceps and urged him back up the length of her body.

Needing to taste her again, to possess her again the way he only could with an honest-to-goodness, mouth-to-mouth, tongue-to-tongue kiss, Chase captured and caressed her lips. Folding her against him, breast to chest, he let her know just how wild she was making him, how hungry. Growling low in his throat, Chase parted her knees and slipped between them, increasingly aware of a need only she could ease. The V of her thighs cradled his hardness and he throbbed against her surrendering softness. They hadn't begun to explore each other—not the way he wanted—but he knew there would be time for that later, and like her he just couldn't wait, didn't want to wait....

As he continued to kiss and caress her, Bridgett trembled as wildly as Chase. So this wasn't what she'd expected, what she'd planned, when she had come here tonight. So what if it wasn't an investment likely to amount to much of anything? She had to have him. Had to be loved, possessed, taken like this. She had to be a part of Chase, at least once in her life. And heaven knew the opportunity might never come again.

So she kissed him back and surged against him, wrapping her legs and arms around him. And when the tip of his manhood pressed against her delicate folds, she moved to receive him, forgetting for a moment the pain, the discomfort, the shock of being one, and gave herself over to the pleasure of loving him with all the passion she possessed. Chase might not love her, she might not ever be loved, but she would have this, Bridgett thought as he drove into her, taking them both to paradise and beyond. And for the moment, for now, it was enough.

BRIDGETT HAD BARELY had time to catch her breath when Chase extricated his body ever so carefully from hers and said, "We have to talk about this."

The matter-of-fact timbre of his tone, coupled with the stunned look on his face, was like being splashed with a bucket of cold water. Chase had wanted her; he just hadn't wanted her to be a virgin. And that, she concluded unhappily, said more about his true feelings for her—or perhaps lack of them— than she really wanted to know.

Not that she should be surprised, Bridgett told herself, unable to help feeling both disappointed and disillusioned by Chase's unhappiness. Hadn't she known that a guy like Chase was only in something like this for a good time? That lovemaking came with a complete lack of responsibility? Except when bedding a virgin she feared. But there was no way she'd allow that in her case, Bridgett decided, determined to salvage her pride.

"No, we don't," Bridgett told Chase with an insouciance she didn't begin to feel.

To her frustration, Chase caught her and pinned her beneath him before she could leave the bed. Not about to let her off that easily apparently, he regarded her in a way that made her blush. "Why didn't you tell me you were a virgin?" he demanded, looking both regretful and annoyed.

Because I knew you would stop if I did. And I didn't want you to stop, Bridgett thought, her heart inundated with a crazy mixture of wonder, confusion and contrition. She had wanted Chase to feel elated that he had been her first. Not be guilty and remorseful.

When she didn't answer him right away, Chase said, "For pity's sake." He sat up in bed, dragging the covers with him to his waist. He reached over and covered her, too. Practically all the way to her chin. His frown deepened as he slanted her a dark accusing look. "You have to know that I would have—"

"Come to your senses and not made love to me at all?" Bridgett interrupted in the most carefree voice she could manage. Really, this remorse of his, on the heels of what had been a truly remarkable lovemaking session, was almost more than she could handle!

Chase leaned back against the headboard and folded his arms in front of him. Was that her imagination, Bridgett wondered, her glance sliding down the sheet drawn across his waist, or was he aroused again?

Aware her throat was suddenly very dry, somewhere else was very wet, and she was beginning to tremble in anticipation of something that probably wasn't going to happen, Bridgett sat up.

Chase cleared his throat. Abruptly his look became one of sadness as he told her gently and sorrowfully, "It's just...I would have done it a little differently if I'd known it was your introduction to lovemaking. I would have gone slower, began more gentle and careful."

What Chase had done, Bridgett thought on a wistful sigh, had been just fine. He had more than met her expectations. He had fulfilled every romantic and sensual dream she had ever had. And therein lay the problem. She was already taking their roll in the rumpled covers of his bed much more seriously than he ever would.

Whereas he was now feeling guilt and anxiety over his behavior, she was head over heels in love.

If that wasn't an out-and-out prescription for a broken heart, Bridgett didn't know what was.

"And you haven't answered my question," Chase continued as Bridgett's misery built to an untenable degree. Chase's blue-gray eyes narrowed in speculation, the guilt he felt about deflowering her still on his face. "How is it possible that you and Martin haven't..." Chase paused as if struggling for the right words. "You were going to marry the guy, Bridgett!"

Well, you're right about one thing, Bridgett thought, feeling pretty darn guilty and upset about her actions, too. *Clearly any thought of accepting a proposal from Martin now is off. There's no way I can marry him now. Not after this. Because this never would have happened if I loved Martin the way I should.*

Aware Chase was still waiting for an answer, and she had one thing left—her pride—Bridgett vaulted out of his bed and tossed back haughtily, "Martin and I didn't make love because Martin didn't try and pressure me into sex, a fact I very much appreciated.''

Chase blinked, his confusion building, instead of lessening. His gaze flicked over her as he stood, too. ''Why the hell not?'' Chase demanded. ''When he's supposed to be in love with you!''

Bridgett's face turned hot with shame as she struggled into her bra and panties. She wished Chase would put on some clothes, too, before they ended up back in bed, making love again. ''Because Martin doesn't think that way.''

''Well, he darn well should,'' Chase stated vehemently, finally reaching for his pants.

Bridgett tried not to feel disappointed as Chase covered his beautiful—and yes, aroused—body from her view. It wasn't hers to admire. Or love. Or want. As much as she might want that to be the case.

''Martin respects me.'' Bridgett stepped into her dress and pulled it up over her hips. And until now, anyway, she thought as she put her arms through the armholes, Martin's hands-off policy had been a good thing. Now, for the first time in her life having made love with a man who truly desired her, Bridgett had to wonder if Martin's disinterest in her sexually was a good thing, after all.

Chase snorted derisively as Bridgett scrambled around looking for her evening sandals. He found them first and handed them to her, then stood back and watched her put them on.

"I respect you, too, Bridgett." Chase stepped behind her and helped her with her zipper. "But that doesn't keep me from wanting to take you to bed. It makes me want to pleasure you all the more."

Just the sound of that and the erotic mental images it conjured up made Bridgett want to make love with Chase all over again. Aware her breath was coming hard and fast—her nipples had already tightened, her middle gone all soft and hot—Bridgett straightened. She did not need to be thinking about how it felt when Chase was deep inside her, driving her toward sweet oblivion. She didn't need to think about the tenderness of his kisses or the wonderful magic of his hands. Or the even more astounding reaction of her body.

Doing her best to appear unaffected by all the frank talk and open declarations of his desire, she squared off with him, chiding, "You're impossible! You know that, don't you?" Suddenly, inexplicably, her throat was clogged with tears. Maybe because she knew this wasn't going to last—Chase's desire for any one woman never did.

"Why?" Chase taunted impatiently, refusing to back down or move away from her. He cupped her shoulders lightly, possessively, the warmth of his palms sending even more sensual messages radiating through her. "Because I'm honest about wanting you?"

Bridgett stared at him despairingly, hardly able to believe she had gotten herself in such a quandary.

She was certainly old enough to know better. Just because something felt right didn't make it right.

"Sex and love are not the same thing," she informed him hoarsely. Her mother had told her that over and over again. And Bridgett had lived long enough, and seen enough of her girlfriends bedded and then abandoned, to know that was true. There were a lot of guys out there who would say and do anything to get a woman into the sack. And until tonight, until he had made love to her as if she was the only woman on earth for him, until she realized that Chase was the only man on earth for her, she had thought Chase was one of them.

Now, because of what she was feeling, Bridgett wasn't one hundred percent certain that was true. Unfortunately she wasn't sure it wasn't true, either. She knew Chase cared about her and always had. But were caring and love the same thing? Or was she just supposed to accept the sex as a new part of their "friendship," and nothing more? The only thing she knew for certain was that she couldn't go on pretending nothing had changed between them, because for her, it had.

"You're right. Sex and love aren't the same," Chase shot back passionately, giving her a look that let her know she was making this unnecessarily hard on them both. "But sex with love is even better," he continued practically. "And caring about someone without taking it to the next level is crazy."

Bridgett studied him warily, weighing everything

he said and did. She was almost afraid to hope, and her heart pounded like a wild thing in her chest. "What are you saying, Chase?" she whispered tremulously.

Chase gazed down at her, his eyes misty, as he spoke the words she wanted so very much to hear. "That I want us to be together, Bridgett. And I know now that I always have."

Chapter Thirteen

"You can't mean that," Bridgett said. Her voice was overflowing with feeling and her eyes were filled with tears.

"The heck I don't," Chase shot back just as emotionally. He cupped her chin in his hand and gently tilted her face up to his. "It took you almost marrying someone else to make me see it," he said, "but I want to be with you, Bridgett. I've wanted that for a very long time. I just wouldn't admit it to myself."

Happiness swept through Bridgett with the force of a tidal wave. "Oh, Chase," she cried, rising on tiptoe and bringing her lips to his, "I want to be with you, too." She kissed him with all the passion and tenderness she possessed. For so long now she had wanted him to yearn for her the way she yearned for him. And yet, as much as she enjoyed the feel of his lips on hers, Bridgett knew they had to pull apart. And talk about this very difficult situation they were in, before their affection for each other went any further. Bridgett splayed her hands across Chase's chest. Like it or not, she knew she and Chase wouldn't be happy until they had cleared the way for the two of them to be together for more than just tonight.

"But that still doesn't mean what we've done here tonight is okay," Bridgett said, determined to make things right. She might not have been engaged to Martin just yet, and she and Martin might not have quite gotten around to making a formal commitment to each other or any promises of exclusivity, but they had been very close to doing all of that. And probably would have, had Bridgett's feelings for Chase not gotten in the way. And so now she was left feeling very upset and guilty. Because she knew now she should have realized Martin wasn't the right man for her and stopped seeing him a long time ago.

Instead, because Martin had offered her the kind of settled married future she wanted, the kind most of the men her own age still didn't, she had kept seeing him. Fooling both of them into thinking that the two of them had a future together that would one day include marriage and children.

And that had been wrong, Bridgett realized, even if she hadn't done any of it deliberately or understood quite what was happening at the time. Or been in something of a blind panic because she was thirty-two and still nowhere near marriage and the children she had always wanted. Because somewhere deep down, she must have known she didn't care about Martin the way she should. Even if she couldn't admit it to herself. Just as she knew she was the marrying kind. And Chase was the kind who would never marry. What was it Chase had said to her? she thought uneasily. *The thought of marriage scares the heck out of me. The thought of making promises I might not be able to keep, well, it's not something I want to do.*

Chase's expression was grim, his concern about the situation evident, too, as he smoothed the hair from her face. "I'm sorry we made love before you had a chance to tell Morganstern you can't and won't see him anymore," Chase told her quietly, then paused and searched her face. "I know that must feel disloyal. But surely you know now that you don't love him and never did. Because if you did, you never would have made love with me tonight."

Bridgett knew that was true. Funny that she hadn't noticed until tonight that she and Martin had never once professed their love for each other. She had just assumed that getting along with and liking each other was enough. She saw now it wasn't.

Hopefully Martin would see things that way, too.

Chase tightened his arms around Bridgett possessively. "You have to tell him the marriage is off."

Bridgett planned to do just that as soon as possible. The problem was how to do it without hurting Martin. Bridgett didn't want to be cruel, and she didn't want to invade her privacy with Chase, either. She swallowed hard and looked up at Chase. "He's going to want an explanation," she warned.

Chase shrugged, less concerned about Martin than he was about her. "Then tell him the truth," Chase advised. "That you and I realized we have feelings for each other, have had them for a long time, and you can't marry him under those conditions. He won't like it," Chase predicted, his eyes narrowing seriously, "but if Martin's half the man you say he is, he'll accept it. And he'll be grateful to you for telling him the truth."

Bridgett's heart pounded in her chest as she faced the uncertainty of her future. "And then what?" she asked warily, very aware that although Chase had made love to her with all the passion and tenderness he possessed, he hadn't actually said he loved her.

Chase tensed. After a moment he dropped his hands, stepped away. "I don't know," he said, still holding her gaze. "I don't usually think that far ahead. But I'm sure we can figure out the best way to handle this," he hastened to assure her.

Her mother was right, Bridgett thought wearily as she studied the conflicting emotions on Chase's face. Love and sex weren't the same thing. Not at all. And she still wasn't the type of woman who could run around having flings and keep her heart intact. Desperation filled her as she took another drink and set her soda can aside. "Listen, I've really got to go." Determined to end the evening now, before the situation deteriorated any further, she brushed by him.

"Now?" Chase followed her out onto the deck.

Bridgett gathered what was left of her dignity and wrapped it around her like a cloak. Love and friendship weren't enough for her. And never would be. Whereas with Chase, well, that was all he wanted. All he probably would ever want. Given that, it was best to end this now, she told herself logically, before their friendship suffered even more irreparable damage. It was going to be hard enough to look him in the eye without remembering all they had done and said. She swallowed around the knot in her throat. "I don't think this should happen again," she said, telling herself it really was for the best.

Chase stared at her as if he had no idea who she was or what she wanted out of life. "You're telling me that's it?" he asked in a low incredulous voice.

Bridgett nodded. And then, unable to say more without bursting into tears, she slipped out the door and made a dash for her car.

BRIDGETT MET MARTIN at the gallery the next morning before it opened.

As soon as he ushered her inside, she said, "I've got something to tell you."

He studied her, taking in her somber navy-blue sheath and upswept hair. "Before you do, I think you should make sure it's something I want to hear."

Her heart pounding uneasily, Bridgett fingered the long strand of pearls around her neck. "What do you mean?"

"We're not children anymore, Bridgett." He took her by the elbow and steered her toward his private office at the rear of the building. As soon as they were inside, he shut the door behind them. "And I'm not as clueless as I sometimes appear."

Bridgett drew a steadying breath, but finding her legs would no longer support her, she dropped down onto the sleek white leather sofa. "You know..." She hesitated.

"That Chase Deveraux has been pursuing you?" Martin shrugged. He poured them both a cup of English tea and brought hers to her. He sat down beside her and swiveled toward her. "I'd have to be a fool not to have seen that," he said as politely and unemotionally as if they'd been discussing the weather.

Bridgett moved back slightly, so that his bent knee was no longer touching her thigh. She looked down at the fine wool of his impeccably tailored suit, still struggling to understand Martin's total lack of emotion about such a serious subject. "Then why didn't you say anything?" she asked.

Martin looked at her even more tranquilly. "Because I didn't think it was necessary."

Bridgett blinked in confusion. She had expected a jealous angry scene, not this cool reaction. "But if...?" She knew Martin was mature, especially in contrast to men her own age. That was one of the things she had always liked about him. But still, she did expect him to be more emotional about the subject of another man.

Martin sipped his tea and gave her a look that was almost pitying. "I don't care if he's made a pass at you, Bridgett," Martin explained matter-of-factly. "I don't care if you've accepted it. I simply don't want to know about it."

The sheer audacity of his view left her momentarily speechless. "You could overlook something like that?" she asked eventually, not sure if she was more disillusioned or disappointed in his lack of true feelings for her.

Martin set his cup aside slowly and deliberately. He unbuttoned his suit coat and leaned back on the sofa once again. "I think if we're going to be married and have children together and stay married, there may be moments when we have to overlook such things. They don't mean anything. I would just expect you to be discreet, as I would be, if the situation ever arose."

"That's a very sophisticated attitude to have," Bridgett said finally.

Martin smiled. "How else do you think the people in my family have managed to stay married and keep their fortunes intact all these years?"

Feeling increasingly foolish because it turned out Chase had been right about Martin, after all, Bridgett stood and began to pace the elegantly appointed room. "You never said anything about this," she murmured, upset. Because if Martin had, she would have stopped seeing him months ago. Before she had wasted all that time. And made such a fool of herself defending him to others, like her mother and Chase, who had sensed all along that there was something just too good to be true about Martin Morganstern. That there was some reason no other woman had deigned to marry him or even get engaged to the forty-five-year-old bachelor.

Martin lifted his hands and let them fall back to his lap. "To be frank, I didn't think it would be a problem. You didn't seem all that passionate a person to me..."

At least until Chase Deveraux came along to show her otherwise, Bridgett amended silently.

"And frankly, I'm not, either," Martin continued pragmatically. He gazed at her with the tenderness and kindness she had once so revered. "And I'm happy about that. I think not being so physical makes life a lot easier. Companionship and understanding are what I'm looking for."

What he was describing was fine in a friend. Just not enough in a spouse.

"Unfortunately I'm not all that understanding," Bridgett stated as she opened her purse. Deciding it was time to call an end to this farce once and for all, she handed Martin a velvet box containing the emerald ring he had given her. "Because I do want fidelity, on both sides. I can't imagine being married without it.''

CHASE HADN'T WANTED to let Bridgett go after they'd made love. He had wanted to keep her there with him all night and move her in with him the next morning. But he had sacrificed his own desire because he had known Bridgett was right about one thing: she had to end it with Martin before her relationship with him went any farther. And she had needed to do it alone. So he had put aside his own irritation at the inexplicable way she had gone so hot and cold on him again and reluctantly let her go with their own future unresolved. That hadn't stopped him from worrying, however. And when she hadn't contacted him by noon the following day or returned any of his calls, he went in search of her. First he wanted to make sure she was okay and that she had broken it off with Martin as she had promised. And second he wanted to understand why she had decided, without consulting him, they shouldn't make love again. He intended to change her mind about that. But first, he had to understand her reasons. And bitter experience told him that was not going to be an easy task.

He found her jogging in Battery Park. Hurriedly he finished stretching and joined her on the path by the seawall. Deciding nothing would be gained by beating around the bush, he plunged right in. ''You've been avoiding me.''

"And I'm going to keep right on avoiding you," Bridgett said, confirming his earlier assumption that he would never understand women and what they wanted, no matter how hard he tried. Bridgett was even more of an enigma to him. But she wouldn't stay an enigma, Chase decided firmly. Not if he had his way.

"And why is that?" he asked easily.

She turned and regarded him then, the look in her eyes so melancholy he was afraid they'd never be friends again, never mind lovers. "You know why," she said softly, and picked up her pace.

Which was, Chase thought, the hell of it. Because now that he was with her again, he did know why. He had handled last night—heck, his whole relationship with her—all wrong! Bridgett deserved romance. Courting. Dates and flowers and surprises. Intimate walks on the beach. Wonderful dinners. And all the courtship rituals that showed a woman she meant something to a man. Instead, what Bridgett had gotten was a roll in the hay. And as passionate and tender as their lovemaking had been, it wasn't enough. Not for her. Unfortunately Chase couldn't take it back. He couldn't give her a better introduction to lovemaking, more suitable to the innocent woman she was, rather than the sophisticate he'd thought her to be. All they could do was move forward. He was more than ready to do that, if she'd only give him a chance.

"I'm sorry about last night," he said eventually,

wishing she'd give him at least half a chance to make it up to her. "If I'd known—"

The flush in Bridgett's cheeks deepened attractively. "Don't apologize," she said quickly. And the impersonal way she looked at him then made him realize he'd do whatever he had to do to keep her from easing out of his life again. "We might not have planned it." Her voice sounded hoarse. Stressed. "But we're both adults," she continued, almost too casually. "We can handle it."

Could they? Chase wondered, noting the hurt in her eyes. He disagreed. "We can't keep avoiding each other."

"Don't you think a little time-out is warranted?" she asked, picking up her speed even more. "I mean, it's not as if talking about it will help anything."

"It would help me," Chase said, beginning to get angry.

"Too bad." She frowned at him. "Because all it's doing is annoying me."

Giving him no chance to answer, Bridgett raced ahead as if trying to leave him way behind. Not about to be pushed away that easily again, Chase picked up his own pace until they were once again running side by side. It didn't matter whether she went faster or slower, he stayed with her. Predictably, bright spots of color that had nothing whatsoever to do with the exertion she was expending, soon appeared in her cheeks.

After a while, figuring his point had been made, Chase turned his glance her way and prepared to resume their conversation. If Bridgett didn't want to talk about the two of them, they'd talk about the rest of her romantic life. He made no effort to disguise his relief as he observed casually, "I heard you and Martin called it quits."

Bridgett's lips tightened as they skirted past a group of professionals enjoying the beautiful spring weather on their lunch break, then went back to running side by side. "Who told you that?" She kept her gaze straight ahead.

Chase slanted her another glance, taking in her Charleston Harbor T-shirt and sunshine-yellow running shorts. "Your mother. She was happy about it."

"Yes—" Bridgett kept her eyes on the cargo ship entering the harbor as if it was the most interesting thing in the world "—I know."

Chase ducked behind Bridgett as they ran past another group of joggers coming the opposite way. "She said she thought you were relieved."

"I am." Bridgett turned off the path abruptly and stopped beneath the shade of a tall palmetto tree. "It turns out you were right about him, after all." She brushed the damp hair from her forehead. "He's not the man for me." Briefly she explained Martin's sophisticated views on infidelity. Views she didn't begin to share. Victory spilled through Chase, followed swiftly by soul-deep satisfaction.

"I knew he had ice water in his veins," Chase stated smugly. Turned out his gut instincts had been right on target, after all.

"So you're off the hook, Chase." Bridgett bent over at the waist, still looking as if she had lost her best friend in the whole world as she worked to catch her breath. She wiped the perspiration from her brow and looked at him meaningfully. "You don't have to feel guilty about breaking the two of us up any longer. You did me a favor." She straightened and spun around, ready to jog off again.

This time Chase grabbed her by the shoulders and prevented her flight. Figuring she'd run far enough, he forced her head up to face him. "I don't feel guilty," he told her flatly, still wishing fervently that their first bout of lovemaking had come about some other way and some other time, when she already believed how very much he cared about her. "And I don't consider what happened between us a favor."

Instead, it had been a revelation. For both of them. And there had been a brief time, just after it had happened, before reality'd had time to sink in and she had panicked and run out on him, when Bridgett had known it and felt it, too.

"Maybe you should consider it another one of those things friends do for each other." Bridgett shrugged out of his light grasp.

"Why?" Chase demanded, tamping down his

hurt, aware it was all he could do not to haul her close and kiss her senseless.

"Because," Bridgett countered just as stubbornly, "you and I both know that it didn't mean anything and it's not going to happen again."

The defiance in her voice was unmistakable. "You can't mean that," Chase said, stunned. His inability to understand women or how they thought, what they felt, had never seemed more pronounced.

Bridgett looked at him as if he didn't know her at all. "Yes," she said softly, and raced off. "I do!"

CHASE FINISHED his run—alone—then went to the one place he figured he could enlist some help, if not with talking sense into Bridgett, at least with understanding her. Because right now the romantic heart of her was as much a mystery to him as ever. And he didn't think he could endure the way she went hot and cold on him for seemingly no reason much longer.

His mother was the first person he saw upon arrival, and she was knee-deep in a rainbow of spring flowers. Grace looked up at him as he walked in and promptly scowled at the sweaty state of his running clothes. She paused, crystal vase in hand. "Don't you dare track dirt in on that floor, Chase Deveraux! If you do, Theresa will have your hide."

"Nice to see you, too, Mom." Chase left his grimy running shoes outside on the back porch and walked on in, blotting his face with the towel he'd slung around his neck. Knowing better than to perch on any of the beautiful wicker furniture in the sunroom in his present state, he headed into the kitchen for a bottle of water from the refrigerator and a wooden chair, and brought them both back to the sunroom. He put the chair down back to front next to his mother and sat. "What are you doing?"

Grace gave him a look that told him he should have had a shower before coming over. "I'm arranging flowers for Bridgett's party tonight."

Chase folded his arms over the chairback and took another long thirsty swallow of water. "You heard she and Martin broke up."

"Yes." Grace snipped the ends off a handful of daffodils, then put one each in the dozen or so vases she had lined up on the folding table, erected for the purpose. Finished, she reached for a handful of buttercups. "Consequently Martin won't be attending this evening."

"A shame," Chase said.

Grace looked up from her snipping. She regarded him steadily. "You don't seem to think so," she remarked dryly.

Chase shrugged, refusing to pretend otherwise. "I never liked the guy," he said flatly.

"From what I've seen, he's a very nice man. Handsome. Polite. Prosperous."

Obviously, Chase thought, Bridgett hadn't told *his* mother Martin's views on marital fidelity.

Knowing Bridgett, she probably hadn't said anything to her own mother, either.

"It takes more than handsome, polite and prosperous to make a good husband," Chase said. It took the kind of love only he could give her. Not that he'd ever get Bridgett to admit that.

"Still, from everything I've heard, Martin really seemed to care for Bridgett," Grace said carefully after a moment.

If you want a husband with ice water running through his veins, Chase conceded sarcastically to himself, *Martin* probably would be a good choice. He studied his mother, wondering just what it was about women and marriage. From what he could tell, the young ones, who had yet to be married, wanted desperately to be hitched. This feeling intensified, the older they got. Hence, Bridgett's attachment to Martin. The ones like his mother who had suffered through a divorce and gone on to build a life alone seemed totally disinterested in tying the knot again or even being that serious about any one man. Deciding to delve into the reasons for that, he asked his mother casually, "Do you think you'll ever get married again?"

Grace looked up, stunned. "To someone other than your father?"

Of course, Chase thought. Unless... Deciding not to beat around the bush, he asked, "Are you considering remarrying Dad?"

Twin spots of color appeared in Grace's cheeks.

"No, of course not," she replied hastily. Finished with the buttercups, she reached for the pink roses.

"How come?" Chase shot back, deciding to use this opportunity to try to find out why his parents had divorced.

"Because I've been there, done that," Grace said briskly.

"What about with someone else, then?" Chase asked.

Grace continued to avert her gaze. "I don't think so, no."

Who not, Chase wondered. "Don't you believe in marriage?" Because, he realized belatedly, he was sure beginning to.

"Yes. Of course I do." Grace stuffed lilies into the mix.

Chase took another swig of water. "Then...?" Chase prodded, sensing there was more.

Grace paused, her beautiful face masked in disillusionment. "If it didn't work out with your father, I don't think it will work out with anyone."

Chase knew what it was like to feel that kind of pain—he was feeling it now with Bridgett. He couldn't really see himself ever marrying anyone else, either. "You really loved Dad, didn't you?" he said after a moment.

Sorrow appeared in his mother's eyes as she readily admitted, "Yes, I did..."

"And Dad loved...loves you," Chase said carefully.

"I believe so, despite our differences." Grace paused and searched Chase's face.

"What would have made you stay with Dad, instead of getting a divorce?"

That, it seemed, was easy.

Grace looked Chase straight in the eye. "If I'd known I was the most important person in his life, above all else—our careers, any difficulties we had, everything. If I'd just known I could count on him to love me the way I needed and wanted to be loved, I would have stayed."

Chapter Fourteen

Bridgett wasn't exactly in a party mood, but given all the trouble her mother and Grace and Winnifred had gone to, to welcome her back to Charleston, there was no way she could avoid the party. So she got herself ready, taking as much care as she would have had she actually been going to see Chase that evening.

Her mother, it seemed, approved of Bridgett's attire, too. "Oh, honey, you look gorgeous!" Theresa enthused when Bridgett stopped by her mother's apartment on the third floor of the Deveraux mansion.

"So do you, Mom," Bridgett returned, the emotional catch in her voice mirroring Theresa's. For once Theresa was going to be a guest at one of Grace and Tom's parties, instead of the housekeeper running things behind the scene. Bridgett had never been prouder of her mother than she was at that moment. Theresa might have had a hard life as a single mother and domestic, but tonight, in a beaded sapphire-blue dress and matching shoes, her red hair swept up in an elegant twist, Theresa looked young and vital and ready for a romance of her own.

Theresa studied Bridgett's reflection in the mirror, knowing, as always, when Bridgett was upset. "Are you worried about people talking about your breakup with Martin?" Theresa asked, concerned.

"No," Bridgett said. And it was true. That kind of gossip she could deal with. It was the damage to her friendship with Chase that had her feeling so sad and uncertain. Because she honestly didn't know where they went from here. Was she right to try to go back to being just friends before any further hurt or disillusionment was inflicted on either of them? Or should she chance it and hope for the best, knowing all the while, because of her background and the fact that she had grown up illegitimate, that she had never been the kind of woman made for casual flings?

"Are you worried about never getting married?" Theresa persisted.

I'm worried about making the same mistakes you made. I'm worried I'm going to give my heart to a man who can't or won't love me back, and then spend the rest of my life regretting my foolishness, Bridgett thought. But not wanting to hurt her mother's feelings, she swallowed and sat down on the edge of Theresa's bed. She smoothed the damask coverlet with her fingertips and chose her words carefully. "I know it's silly. Childish of me, really.

But I always thought, growing up, that there was going to be this one man out there for me whom I would love above all else. And that he would come along and sweep me off my feet and make me his bride, and we'd have children together and live happily ever after.'' She'd thought—even more foolishly—that her knight would be Chase. And worse, now that she had crossed that bridge and made love with him, she knew she would never care for any man the way she cared for Chase.

"I know how you feel, honey." Theresa moved around the end of the four-poster to sit down beside Bridgett. "I had the same dream."

"Only, it didn't come true for you." Bridgett swallowed around the lump in her throat, for the first time understanding the pain her mother must have suffered when her love affair ended. She must have been devastated. "Simon Oglethorpe left you."

"And you," Theresa reminded Bridgett gently, taking her hand in both of hers. "And I have to worry if that didn't scar you, just a bit, despite everything I tried to do to protect you."

Bridgett had always appreciated her mother's honesty and efforts to do right by her. "You told me the way it was," she countered stubbornly, tightly clasping her mother's work-worn hand.

Theresa sighed heavily. "And in the process left you looking for someone mature and reliable who was never going to make you as truly happy as you deserved to be, instead of that one true passionate love of your life." She stood and moved away, her heels clicking on the wood floor. Then she turned back to Bridgett, sorrow in her eyes. "I fear I did you a disservice, asking you to judge a man's trustworthiness by his bank account or lack thereof and warning you away from romance." Regret colored her low voice. "There's no reason we both should be paying for my mistake in choosing the wrong man, who just happened to be self-centered and wealthy, because that's exactly what you've been doing, Bridgett. Putting too much weight on the facts of a man's life that we can all see and admire, and not enough store in your own feelings."

Bridgett studied the love in her mother's eyes. "You're telling me to take more chances, aren't you," she asked softly.

Theresa nodded. "I'm telling you to follow your heart, honey."

And Bridgett knew what her heart was telling her to do.

HE WAS LATE. And he was never late. Bridgett walked over to Gabe, aware the party had been going on for a full three hours now and Chase had yet to appear. This was not a good sign. She smiled at his handsome younger brother. "Did you hear from Chase today?" Bridgett asked. She hoped the two of them hadn't had another argument, one that would preclude Chase's coming to the party tonight.

"No." Gabe looked at Bridgett, taking in her stunning dress and elegantly upswept hair. "You?"

Bridgett sipped a little of her champagne, but passed on the canapés being circulated by white-coated waiters from the catering company. She turned back to Gabe. "I saw him earlier jogging in the park," Bridgett admitted.

"I gather he didn't say anything then about skipping the party," Gabe said.

"No." But she'd made it pretty clear to Chase that he was no longer welcome in her life, Bridgett recalled ruefully. What a fool she had been. Pushing Chase away when all he had wanted was to be close to her.

"Sorry about you and Morganstern," Gabe continued.

"That's okay. It was for the best," Bridgett said, and meant it. She felt nothing but relief. And gratitude to Chase for forcing her to see what she would rather not have admitted—that she was with Martin out of fear and desperation, rather than love. And those were not reasons anyone should marry, have children and try to build a life together.

"You'll find the right man someday," Gabe said.

I already have, Bridgett thought as a hush fell over the crowd. Bridgett and Gabe turned toward the door. Chase walked in, his former fiancée, Maggie Callaway, on his arm. And Bridgett felt her heart sink clear to the floor.

CHASE COULD SEE Bridgett was taking this the wrong way. But given the fact that all eyes were now upon them, he had no choice but to take Maggie all the way over to Gabe.

"Maybe this wasn't such a good idea," Maggie Callaway whispered to Chase.

"Trust me, it's a great idea," Chase said, holding on to Maggie more tightly and refusing to let her drag her feet. He should have done this two years ago. Think of all the heartbreak and humiliation, not to mention family tensions, he would have avoided if he had just bothered to own up to his own short-comings and talk to Gabe. Chase and Maggie stopped just short of Gabe and Bridgett. Not surprisingly, Gabe looked fit to be tied and jealous as all get-out. "I believe you owe this lady a dance," Chase told Gabe, inclining his head to the moonlit garden beyond.

Bridgett looked at Chase as if he was crazy. "There's no music outside," she protested.

"So they'll make some," Chase said. He took Bridgett's arm in his, as a visibly stunned Gabe and a trembling Maggie wandered off outside, looking as if they had a lot to say to each other, as well.

Bridgett looked incredibly beautiful in some sort of shimmery gold gown with a halter top and close-fitting bodice, and a skirt that fluffed out at her waist before falling in a whisper-soft circle to her knees. The fabric was very soft, and so was all the exposed skin on her back, shoulders and in the V neckline, Chase thought. She'd swept up her hair into a loose tumble of auburn curls and put on a gold necklace and earrings that perfectly accented the dress. Chase didn't need to edit a magazine to know she had taken an extraordinary amount of time dressing for the evening. As had he.

"I didn't think you were coming," Bridgett said in a low voice.

"Then you have a lot to learn about me and how relentless I can be when I want something," Chase said. And right now he wanted Bridgett more than anything he'd ever wanted in his life. He could only hope that by the time morning came, she'd feel the same. If not, he'd just have to work harder at bringing her around. "I've decided we're going to refocus our priorities."

Bridgett's gaze trailed slowly over his black tux before returning slowly and deliberately to his face. Too late, Chase recalled she had never liked being told what to do or how to behave. "And if I don't agree?" she murmured mischievously, giving him a saucy look. "Then what?"

Chase inclined his head at her. "Then we'll keep talking until you do," he said.

A challenging light sparkled in her eyes and a smug smile curved her lips. "Confident, aren't you?"

"Resolute," Chase said, knowing this was one battle of the sexes he would win. "And with good reason." An awful lot was at stake. And this time he wasn't going to screw things up. This time he was going to hang in there and do whatever it took to make sure he understood Bridgett, heart and soul. No more chalking up their differences to the mysteries of the female psyche and walking away. From now on, his first order of business was making sure he met all the needs of the woman in his life.

Impatiently he looked toward the foyer again, wondering what was taking so long. A second later his aunt Winnifred moved away from the window and bustled toward the door. She opened it as previously planned, revealing a Rolls-Royce limousine idling at the curb. "That's our ride." Chase plucked the champagne glass from Bridgett's hand.

"What do you mean, 'our ride'?" Bridgett asked.

"You'll see." Grinning, Chase put an arm beneath her knees and scooped her up in his arms. The guests laughed and clapped while Bridgett flushed from head to toe.

"For heaven's sake! Put me down," Bridgett demanded as Chase strode with her down the walk to the waiting car.

"Okay." But Chase waited until a tuxedo-clad Harry, Winnifred's butler, had opened the limo door before he set Bridgett on the plush leather seat and pushed his way in after her. The butler closed the car door behind them and then circled around to climb behind the wheel.

Bridgett settled back against the seat opposite Chase and folded her arms in front of her. "I don't know what you think you're doing!" she said breathlessly as the car pulled away from the curb and headed for the prearranged destination. "Carting me off, caveman-style!"

Chase grinned at Bridgett, loving the passion in her voice and eyes—it was something he planned to see every day for the rest of their lives. "Yes, you do," he replied smugly.

"You just let everyone at that party know that we...that we're..." Bridgett sputtered irately.

"Yeah," Chase said with satisfaction as he slid across to sit beside her. For as long as he lived, he would remember the look in her eyes as she realized he had come to claim her as his. "I sure did. And you know what? You loved every romantic second of it."

Bridgett opened her mouth to disagree, then clamped it shut again. "Since when did you get so demonstrative?" she demanded after a moment.

Deciding she was still too far away, Chase pulled her over onto his lap. "Since you came back into my life in a very different but very important way."

Bridgett splayed her hands across his chest and looked deep into his eyes. "You're planning to make love to me tonight, aren't you?" she asked softly.

Chase's pulse kicked into overdrive as he thought about the upcoming evening. "And then some," he said.

Chapter Fifteen

Bridgett would have preferred an immediate seduction, one that gave her no time to think. She should have known that wasn't Chase's plan. Whatever happened between them was not going to be ill thought out this time. He wanted to know if they could be lovers and still be friends. He wanted a decision from her about their future. Finality. No impetuous decisions that would wrench them apart again. Bridgett knew what her decision was. Was it too much to hope that Chase's decision was identical?

His expression as serious as her thoughts, Chase nodded at the window. "Here we are."

Bridgett turned and saw they had arrived at the marina and had parked in front of the boat slip that held the *Endeavor,* the sleek Deveraux yacht. Harry opened the door, Chase took Bridgett by the hand and led her toward the gangway. "Everything's all set for you," Harry said.

"Thanks," Chase said.

Bridgett didn't even have to ask if Chase could pilot the vessel. He and all his siblings had learned to navigate all matter of watercraft from the time they were teens. Inside, the yacht was lit with candles and decorated with pastel roses. Chase led her to the helm and then took his place behind the wheel.

"You'll have to give me a minute to get out of here," he said, his attention momentarily diverted as he started the yacht.

"And then what?" Bridgett asked.

"Then we'll talk," Chase promised.

It took a good twenty minutes to get out into the ocean and drop anchor. As soon as they did, Chase cut the engine, took her by the hand and led her to the stateroom, where a bottle of champagne on ice and a sumptuous meal were waiting. Chase's expression was serious as he took her wrist and clasped it warmly. "I know I've never lived this way, Bridgett, but I can give you this kind of life. Between my trust fund and what I earn at the magazine, we could have a dozen homes and as many different kinds of watercraft and cars as you want."

"Oh, Chase." Bridgett sighed, realizing Chase thought a big part of what had attracted her to Martin Morganstern had been his enormous family wealth and elegant lifestyle. "Money was never what I wanted from you. You could live out at the beach at your place and I could live in town at mine, and I'd still be perfectly happy." *As long as I knew you loved me and always would. As long as I knew the two of us would always and forever be there for each other.*

"I don't think that would work for me, the two of us living in two different places. I'm going to be very demanding," Chase told her soberly. "I'm going to want the two of us under one roof. And I'm not about to ask us both to look the other way while we each have our discreet little affairs. There's only going to be one man in your bed, and that's going to be me."

The possessiveness in his blue-gray eyes stole her breath away. "It sounds like you're staking a claim," Bridgett murmured. A pretty long-term claim.

"You better believe I am."

The next thing Bridgett knew, she was in his arms again and he was kissing her with all the tenderness and passion she had ever wanted. She shifted closer, wrapped her arms around his neck and kissed him back with all the love she had in her heart.

Finally, when she was breathless and aching, he scooped her up in his arms and carried her to a bedroom that looked as if it had had no preparation at all, save the usual cleaning. "You didn't turn down the bed?" Bridgett teased as he set her down next to it.

"No way was I hedging my bets." Chase slipped off his tuxedo jacket, his cummerbund and tie. "Besides, I'm not in a hurry tonight."

Her mouth dry, Bridgett watched as he unfastened the first two buttons of his shirt, kicked off his shoes.

"You're very beautiful," he murmured as he took her back in his arms and kissed his way down her neck. "Have I told you that?"

Bridgett's heart pounded with anticipation of the lovemaking to come. "So are you." He felt so good against her, so warm and strong and solid.

"And soft. Especially here." He unclasped the back of her dress and slipped his hand beneath the halter top and bra, gently cupping and caressing her breast. He rubbed his hands across her nipples until she sucked in her breath. He covered her breasts with both palms and massaged them until she trembled. Then he fit his lips around the tip of one breast and suckled lightly until she strained against him. Wanting more. Wanting everything. Bridgett threaded her hands through his hair, holding him close, wanting his slow sensual possession of her never to stop.

He came back up to kiss her thoroughly, taking her mouth in a slow mating dance. He kissed her until she, too, was treating each kiss like a beginning and an end in itself, until she was so aroused she could barely breathe. She moved her hips, rubbing against him. She was so empty inside. So tired of being without him.

"And soft…here…" His other hand lifted her skirt and moved to the inside of her thigh.

Bridgett swayed as he slipped his palm inside her panties. And found her, silky wet. Aware they had just begun to make love to each other and she was already on the brink, she slid a hand inside the waist of his trousers and touched him, too. "And you're...not!"

Rather, he was hard as a rock, hot and velvety smooth. Just touching him that way made her want him deep inside her. But he wasn't to be rushed, she realized, as Chase stayed her hand and drew both her wrists behind her. Unfastened her earrings and set them aside.

He kissed both lobes and then made his way leisurely down the slope of her neck, feathering kisses, taking his time, making sure she understood they were going to do this his way, in his time. "I meant what I said about slowing things down, giving you the kind of loving you should have had the first time," Chase murmured as he unbuttoned and opened his shirt with his free hand, then rubbed his chest across her bared breasts, tantalizing her budding nipples with the silky mat of chest hair and hard muscle beneath.

"How about fast now and slow later?" she whispered back, bringing her lips back to his for another slow, sensual, searing kiss.

He eased her back onto the bed, even as she trembled fervently. His smile was wickedly determined and full of the need to please. "I don't think so."

"Chase..." Sensations hammered at her.

He undressed her slowly, kissing each newly bared expanse of skin. She arched against him as he lingered over her breasts and her thighs and every sweet inch in between. "We've got all night. And this time," he murmured as he clasped her hips in his hands and held her steady, "I won't be rushed." And with that, he set about showing her just how thorough he could be. She offered him whatever he wanted from her, whatever he needed, and she took, too, even as she surged toward the outer limits of her control and beyond.

"I love you, Bridgett," he whispered as she undressed and loved him, too, until he was trembling and just as feverish as she.

"I love you, too, Chase," she whispered back. More than she had ever dreamed possible. Then he was pushing her thighs apart with his knees, lifting her hips and sliding a pillow beneath them. She was shaking with a fierce unquenchable ache. She rocked against him, every part of her wanting every part of him. He kissed her in ways that revealed his soul. He kissed her until she was lost in him, in this. And then he was stroking her gently again with his hands, finding the soft feminine center of her, easing the way. She moaned, wanting to feel connected to him, all the way, not just physically, but heart and soul. And then, at long last, they were one. Moving together, surely, sensually. And he was letting her know, with every deep passionate thrust, that he wanted her every bit as wildly as she wanted him.

Her heart soaring at the love and the intimacy and pleasure she'd found, Bridgett wrapped her arms and legs around him, brought him closer and arching her back, pulled him deeper still. And then there was no more holding back. They were soaring. Shaking. He was so deeply buried in her that they were one, free-falling into ecstasy.

BRIDGETT WASN'T SURE how long it took them to come back down to earth and regain their breaths. She only knew she felt so cozy and right lying there wrapped in his arms that she never wanted to move again. But eventually, of course, they did. Chase eased his weight off her and rolled onto his side. He slid a hand beneath her back, hooked a leg over both of hers and looked down at her, all the love she had ever wanted to see in his eyes.

"I know we talked about marriage," Chase said, taking her hand in his.

Bridgett silenced him with a finger to his lips, wary of anything that might spoil this special moment. "We don't have to talk about that, Chase," she told him seriously, meaning the words with every fiber of her being. "Not anymore. Because I've changed my mind." She was ready now to make some sacrifices, too. "I don't need a ring on my finger or a legal document telling me how you feel." All she had to do was look in his eyes, feel the way he loved her, to know how much he cared for her and always would. "All I need is for us to be together, whenever, however we can be together." The details of which she was sure they would work out over time.

Chase studied her, amazed and pleased. "You mean that, don't you," he murmured.

Bridgett nodded. "With all my heart." To prove it, she kissed him again, sweetly and tenderly, surrendering fully to the love that was in her soul, the love that now bound them together. She had never really trusted a man until now. And the way she trusted Chase, with her future and her happiness, left her feeling wonderful and free of the burden of fear she had carried for so long. She didn't know exactly how things would work out. She just knew that they would.

Chase regarded her affectionately as he threaded a hand through her hair. "There's only one problem with that, Bridgett," he told her. A sentimental smile curved his lips. "I don't want us to simply live together. And I sure as heck don't want us living apart. So that means—" he untangled their bodies and reached over to get something from the bedside-table drawer "—we're going to have to make it official as soon as possible." He folded a velvet ring box into her palm and kissed the back of her hand. "Marry me, Bridgett, and make me the happiest man on this whole planet."

Bridgett's eyes filled with tears and a wave of tenderness washed over her. She'd never felt so happy in her life or so full of hope for their future.

"Of course I'll marry you," she said as Chase fit the beautiful diamond ring on the ring finger of her left hand. And their futures pledged, their hearts full of love and wonder, they set about making love all over again.

Epilogue

A week later the whole family and guests gathered on the deck of the *Endeavor*. They took the yacht out into the harbor and dropped anchor just off Fort Sumter, with Chase's beach house in view. There, beneath the brilliant South Carolina sun, Chase and Bridgett joined hands beneath an arbor of pastel roses, looked deep into each other's eyes and made the love they shared official.

"I, Bridgett, take thee Chase…"

"To have and to hold…from this day forward…"

"In sickness and in health…as long as we both shall live…"

The minister beamed down at them. "You may kiss the bride."

Chase wrapped her in his arms and kissed her with all the love he had in his heart. Bridgett kissed him back just as passionately. As they drew apart, the guests erupted in cheers and applause. "How does it feel to be Mrs. Chase Deveraux?" Chase teased.

"Every bit as good as it does for you to be my husband." Bridgett winked.

"How about a picture of the entire family?" Daisy Templeton asked, camera in hand.

Chase wrapped his arm around Bridgett's shoulders. As everyone lined up, he couldn't help but note that Maggie Callaway was talking a lot to Gabe, although they still didn't look as if they were together. But his parents, strangely enough, were hardly talking at all. In fact, in their unguarded moments, he couldn't ever remember seeing them so tense. Which was pretty strange, since this was a very happy occasion and he knew they both approved wholeheartedly of his marriage, as they'd told him so repeatedly in the past few days. Which meant it had to be something else causing the tension between Tom and Grace.

"Everything okay?" Chase asked his mother when they had a moment alone.

Grace smiled. "Of course. I'm very happy for you and Bridgett."

"But...?" Chase prodded.

Grace merely squeezed his arm and moved away. Subject closed.

Frustrated to find his parents still not able to completely work out their differences, whatever the heck they were, Chase turned to his dad. "Did you and Mom have a fight?"

"Fight?" Tom blinked, stunned by both the premise and the question. "No."

"Then what's going on between you two?" Chase persisted.

Tom was silent a moment as he stared down at his champagne. Finally he confided, "Weddings have been hard for us since our divorce. I guess they remind us of our own failure. But your mother and I are happy for you and Bridgett, Chase. Very happy."

Chase could see that, just as he could see something else was going on. Something neither of his parents wanted him to know.

He also knew, whatever the answer, the mystery would not be solved tonight. So he put it aside, accepted his father's good wishes and moved across the deck. Maybe his parents would get back together yet. But whatever happened, Chase knew it was going to take time. His heart full of hope for the future, he returned to his new bride. Bridgett was seated next to Mitch and laughing at something his sister, Amy, said. As Chase reflected on the events leading up to the wedding, he realized that Amy had seemed pretty happy, if a little wistful at times. Which made sense. She had never made a secret of wanting a family of her own. She just hadn't found the right guy. But Mitch had not seemed happy at all. Maybe it was because Mitch had recently been through a bitter divorce. Or maybe, Chase thought, something else was bringing Mitch's spirits down. Like a problem at work. Chase knew Mitch wanted a more important role in the family shipping company than simply being one of the vice presidents on his father's executive staff. But with Tom still so young and vital and immersed in the business, it wasn't likely to happen soon. Tom probably wouldn't hand over the reins of the family company to Mitch for another ten or fifteen years, at the earliest.

"You don't have to pity me," Mitch said to Chase as he stood to let Chase sit down at the table.

"I wasn't—"

"Yeah, you were," Mitch said, looking Chase straight in the eye. He touched his shoulder. "And it's not necessary. I'm fine. You just pay attention to your new bride."

"What was that about?" Bridgett said when Chase sat down and Mitch moved off.

Chase grinned. "Some guy thing. Not to worry. He'll work it out." And he knew Mitch would, too, because Mitch had Deveraux blood in him, and the Deveraux were one hardy, resilient bunch.

After dinner the yacht motored back to shore. The guests disembarked, and then Chase and Bridgett took the yacht back out to sea and dropped anchor. "Alone at last," Chase teased as he took Bridgett in his arms.

"And not a moment too soon." Bridgett stood on tiptoe, wreathed her arms about his neck and kissed him tenderly. "I love you, Chase Deveraux," she whispered softly.

"And I love you, Bridgett. With all my heart."

They kissed again, and then hand in hand, turned to go below.

Their wedding-night lovemaking was as tender and passionate as Bridgett could ever have wished. Arm in arm, they went aloft to watch the dawn. There, in the mists hovering above the water, was the specter of a beautiful young woman in white. She was unmistakably a Deveraux. And her ghostly image disappeared almost as soon as it appeared.

"Eleanor," Chase said.

"I'd say it was our imagination if not for this." Bridgett picked up one of a dozen or more red rose petals scattered across the deck of the yacht and a faded card, with the words "A Love that Lasts Forever" written across its front. Inside the card was one word—"Mitch."

"What do you think this means?" Bridgett asked Chase as a chill breeze moved across the deck and sent her into his arms.

Chase held Bridgett close. "I don't know," he said, studying the beautifully penned script with a frown. "Unless..."

"What?" Bridgett asked, her heart pounding as she clung to Chase.

Chase shrugged and guessed, "Mitch is next."

Beginning in October from

HARLEQUIN®

AMERICAN *Romance*®

TRADING PLACES

A brand-new duo from popular Harlequin authors

RITA HERRON
and
DEBRA WEBB

When identical twin brothers decide to trade lives, they get much more than they bargained for!

Available October 2002

THE RANCHER WORE SUITS
by Rita Herron
Rugged rancher Ty Cooper uses his down-home charms to woo beautiful pediatrician Jessica.

Available November 2002

THE DOCTOR WORE BOOTS
by Debra Webb
Ty's next-door neighbor Leanne finds herself falling for sophisticated and sexy Dr. Dex Montgomery.

Available at your favorite retail outlet.

HARLEQUIN®
Makes any time special®

If you enjoyed what you just read,
then we've got an offer you can't resist!

Take 2 bestselling
love stories FREE!
Plus get a FREE surprise gift!

Clip this page and mail it to Harlequin Reader Service®

IN U.S.A.	**IN CANADA**
3010 Walden Ave.	P.O. Box 609
P.O. Box 1867	Fort Erie, Ontario
Buffalo, N.Y. 14240-1867	L2A 5X3

YES! Please send me 2 free Harlequin American Romance® novels and my free surprise gift. After receiving them, if I don't wish to receive anymore, I can return the shipping statement marked cancel. If I don't cancel, I will receive 4 brand-new novels every month, before they're available in stores! In the U.S.A., bill me at the bargain price of $3.99 plus 25¢ shipping & handling per book and applicable sales tax, if any*. In Canada, bill me at the bargain price of $4.74 plus 25¢ shipping & handling per book and applicable taxes**. That's the complete price and a savings of at least 10% off the cover prices—what a great deal! I understand that accepting the 2 free books and gift places me under no obligation ever to buy any books. I can always return a shipment and cancel at any time. Even if I never buy another book from Harlequin, the 2 free books and gift are mine to keep forever.

154 HDN DNT7
354 HDN DNT9

Name _____ (PLEASE PRINT)

Address _____ Apt.# _____

City _____ State/Prov. _____ Zip/Postal Code _____

* Terms and prices subject to change without notice. Sales tax applicable in N.Y.
** Canadian residents will be charged applicable provincial taxes and GST.
   All orders subject to approval. Offer limited to one per household and not valid to current Harlequin American Romance® subscribers.
   ® are registered trademarks of Harlequin Enterprises Limited.

AMER02 ©2001 Harlequin Enterprises Limited

Princes...Princesses...
London Castles...New York Mansions...
To live the life of a royal!

In 2002, Harlequin Books lets you escape to a world of royalty with these royally themed titles:

Temptation:
January 2002—*A Prince of a Guy* (#861)
February 2002—*A Noble Pursuit* (#865)

American Romance:
The Carradignes: American Royalty (Editorially linked series)
March 2002—*The Improperly Pregnant Princess* (#913)
April 2002—*The Unlawfully Wedded Princess* (#917)
May 2002—*The Simply Scandalous Princess* (#921)
November 2002—*The Inconveniently Engaged Prince* (#945)

Intrigue:
The Carradignes: A Royal Mystery (Editorially linked series)
June 2002—*The Duke's Covert Mission* (#666)

Chicago Confidential
September 2002—*Prince Under Cover* (#678)

The Crown Affair
October 2002—*Royal Target* (#682)
November 2002—*Royal Ransom* (#686)
December 2002—*Royal Pursuit* (#690)

Harlequin Romance:
June 2002—*His Majesty's Marriage* (#3703)
July 2002—*The Prince's Proposal* (#3709)

Harlequin Presents:
August 2002—*Society Weddings* (#2268)
September 2002—*The Prince's Pleasure* (#2274)

Duets:
September 2002—*Once Upon a Tiara/Henry Ever After* (#83)
October 2002—*Natalia's Story/Andrea's Story* (#85)

Celebrate a year of royalty with Harlequin Books!

Available at your favorite retail outlet.

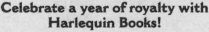

 HARLEQUIN®
Makes any time special ®

Visit us at www.eHarlequin.com

Say "I do" with

HARLEQUIN®

AMERICAN *Romance®*

and

Kara Lennox

How to Marry **A HARDISON**

**First you tempt him. Then you tame him...
all the way to the altar.**

PLAIN JANE'S PLAN
October 2002

Plain Jane Allison Crane knew her chance had finally
come to catch the eye of her lifelong crush, Jeff Hardison.
With a little help from a friend—and one great big
makeover—could Allison finally win her heart's desire?

Don't miss the other titles in this series:

VIXEN IN DISGUISE
August 2002

SASSY CINDERELLA
December 2002

HARLEQUIN®
Makes any time special ®